GHOST FOREST

Advance praise for **GHOST FOREST**

"Moving . . . Bracing fragments and poignant vignettes come together to make a stunning and evocative whole."

—*Publishers Weekly* (starred review)

"*Ghost Forest* is an exceptional debut—risky, precise, witty, and beautiful. How can a painting be distilled into "a single line," or love take root without a home to ground it? Pik-Shuen Fung creates an almost transparent yet weighted world made of relations. This is a moving, alive, and unforgettable book."

—MADELEINE THIEN, author of *Do Not Say We Have Nothing*

"*Ghost Forest* is a debut certain to turn your heart. With a dexterity and style all her own, Fung renders the many voices that make up a family, as well as the mythologies we create for those we know, and those we wish we knew better. I am madly in love with this book, a kaleidoscopic wonder."

—T KIRA MADDEN, author of *Long Live the Tribe of Fatherless Girls*

"Like a Chinese ink painting, every line in Fung's *Ghost Forest* is full of movement and spirit, revealing the resilient threads of matrilineal history and the inheritance of stories and silences. With humor, compassion, and clear-eyed prose, Fung reminds us that grief, memory, and history are never linear but always alive. Fung writes about the questions we forget to ask, the stories that are hidden from us, and the complex acts of care at the core of family. She reminds us that what is unspoken is never lost. *Ghost Forest* is an intimate act of recording and reckoning. It trusts us to listen. It shows us all the languages for love."

—K-MING CHANG, author of *Bestiary*

"In *Ghost Forest*, Fung gives us a family so aching with tenderness, so incandescent with grief and love, that reading about them felt like reading about my own deepest and most secret longings and regrets. This is a book to break your heart and then fill it to bursting again. What an exquisite, glorious debut."

—CATHERINE CHUNG, author of *The Tenth Muse*

"With a single line, you can paint the ocean," says an art teacher in *Ghost Forest*, as apt a description as any for Fung's spare, gorgeous, devastating debut novel. Here, silences speak. Brilliant and pitiless at first, *Ghost Forest* mutates in the reader's hand, until it shimmers with grace and unexpected humor. A mercurial meditation on love and family."

—PADMA VISWANATHAN, author of *The Ever After of Ashwin Rao*

"Made by an artist who angles her mirror to make room for the faces of others, Fung's *Ghost Forest* resembles a xieyi painting, a place where white space and absence are as important as color and life. At once an elegy to all that's been lost between countries, languages, generations, and a quietly urgent call to love what we have. Inventive, funny, and devastating."

—JENNIFER TSENG, author of *Mayumi and the Sea of Happiness*

I put it down on paper and then the ghost does not ache so much.

—SANDRA CISNEROS, *The House on Mango Street*

GHOST FOREST

GHOST FOREST

A NOVEL

Pik-Shuen Fung

 ONE WORLD
New York

Copyright © 2021 by Pik-Shuen Fung

Published in the United States by One World, an imprint of Random House, a division of Penguin Random House LLC, New York.

ONE WORLD and colophon are registered trademarks of Penguin Random House LLC.

Brief portions of this work were published in *The Margins* in 2016.

Hardback ISBN 978-0-593-23096-1
Ebook ISBN 978-0-593-23097-8

Printed in Canada on acid-free paper

oneworldlit.com
randomhousebooks.com

9 8 7 6 5 4 3 2 1

FIRST EDITION

Book design by Simon M. Sullivan

for my grandmother

for my mother

and in memory of my father

BIRD

Twenty-one days after my dad died, a bird perched on the railing of my balcony. It was brown. It stayed there for a long time.

Hi Dad, I said. Thanks for checking up on me.

I lay down on the couch and read some emails on my phone. When I looked up again, the bird was gone.

乖

In my family, the best thing a child could be was gwaai. It meant you were good. It meant you did as you were told.

When I was four, or maybe six, I found out I was supposed to have a baby brother. But my mom said the baby flew to the sky, and that was why my dad was sad those days.

But why is he sad? I asked.

Because he's a traditional Chinese father and he wants to have a son. Try to cheer him up.

Okay, I said.

I decided I would be so gwaai, I would be more perfect than a son.

I was three and a half when we immigrated to Canada. Like many other families, we left Hong Kong before the 1997 Handover. They say almost a sixth of the city left during this time.

My dad had seen news stories of Hong Kongers who couldn't find jobs in their new countries, stories of managers who became dishwashers because they couldn't speak the new language. Like many other fathers, my dad decided he didn't want to leave his job in manufacturing behind.

To help my mom, my grandma and grandpa agreed to move with us to Canada. That spring, my dad took two weeks off from work, and the five of us headed to Kai Tak airport. All my aunts and uncles came to the departure gates to see us off.

In Canada there were more Hong Kong immigrants than in any other country, and in Vancouver, I had many classmates whose fathers stayed in Hong Kong for work too. I didn't think of my family as different. I thought, this is what Hong Kong fathers do.

Astronaut family. It's a term invented by the Hong Kong mass media. A family with an astronaut father—flying here, flying there.

SO FRESH

As we walked out of the arrivals at the Vancouver airport, our family friends waved their arms.

Isn't the air so fresh in Canada? they said.

For two weeks, we stayed at their house in the Richmond neighborhood, and they drove us everywhere. We ate dim sum in Aberdeen Centre, a new mall known as Little Hong Kong, and posed for pictures in Stanley Park, feeding breadcrumbs to the geese. But mostly, we were jet-lagged, riding in the back of their beige minivan, asleep with open mouths.

Two weeks later, after we moved into our new house, they drove us back to the Vancouver airport, where my mom looked at me and said, Say bye-bye to your dad now, he's flying back to Hong Kong.

Through the windows of our new house, I saw plump pointy trees and blurry swishing trees. Everywhere outside was green.

At night, my mom slept in her bedroom, my grandpa in his. I shared a room with my grandma since we were always together. Three generations under one roof.

Dik lik dak lak diklikdaklak diklikdaklak

In our new house in Vancouver, everywhere outside was rain.

CHINATOWN

On weekends, my grandparents, my mom, and I rode the bus to Chinatown to see the herbalist because in Canada we felt always cold.

Afterward, we huddled along the market stalls on Keefer and Main, buying bok choy and hairy gourd, watercress and salted duck kidneys, pork bones and silkie chickens for soup. We shopped enough for the week, and then with a bag in each hand, we rode the bus home.

But over the years, as more and more Hong Kongers moved to Richmond, as Asian supermarkets like Yaohan and T&T opened their doors, as my mom learned to drive and bought us a car, we didn't go to Chinatown anymore.

One time, at the food court in Aberdeen Centre, a woman sat down near us with a steaming bowl of wonton soup. My mom looked twice.

You immigrated? my mom said to the woman.

You also immigrated? the woman said back.

The woman once worked in the same building as my mom in Hong Kong.

ANOTHER SCENE AT THE MALL

Another time, in an aisle of Zellers department store, my mom and her friend pointed at electric water kettles.

How about this one? my mom said.

How about that one? her friend said.

A stranger marched over to say, You Chinese are too loud!

MY PRESCHOOL TEACHER CALLS

One day my preschool teacher called to say, Your daughter goes to the bathroom every two hours.

So my mom took me to the doctor and we did some urine tests, but the results came back normal. The doctor said maybe I was nervous because of the changes, maybe I didn't know how to adapt because I was small, or maybe I didn't have the words.

My grandma says that when I was in preschool in Hong Kong, I always got in trouble for being too loud. All I remember is that, after moving to Canada, every report card said I was too quiet.

MY BEAUTIFUL NOSE

To keep warm, my grandma and I practiced the eighteen forms of qigong in the living room.

Wherever the hand moves, she said, pushing the air with her palm, it knows when it's time to turn.

I turned my palm to my face as if an invisible string attached it to my nose.

Beautiful, my grandma said. When you were a baby, I told your father, My granddaughter is so beautiful! But he said to me, Her nose is too flat! So, for nine months, on the first and the fifteenth of every lunar month, I pinched your nose. Now you have such a beautiful nose. It wasn't like that when you were born.

When I was born, my parents didn't name me. They waited two weeks to see a fortune teller, to ask for an auspicious name.

Looking down at my birth chart the fortune teller said, Her power is very strong. I'm afraid she might squash the son that you want. Find her a godmother to soften it.

My parents thought of a kind Japanese woman they knew through work who didn't have any children. She spoke no English or Cantonese, and lived in the Ibaraki Prefecture. My mom says there is no concept of godmother in Japanese culture, but my godmother accepted right away. To adopt me as her goddaughter, she gave me a pair of chopsticks and a bowl.

But I remember, as I got older, putting my palms together and praying for a sister.

The first character of my name is a generation name, so all the women on my dad's side of the family have it too.

It means green, but not just green—it's the green blue of emeralds.

And the second character means beautiful jade.

THE GREEN CARPET

For a time after we immigrated to Vancouver and before my mom learned she was pregnant again, my grandparents flew back to Hong Kong.

Without my grandma to cook for us, every night my mom and I walked to the local Cantonese restaurant for dinner. Without my grandpa to watch over me, my mom took me to the community center after school. She signed me up for art classes, like pottery and animation, and sat with me in the library for story time.

I still remember the long low shelves where I placed my clay cups before they went into the kiln, the click-click of the projector in the dark dusty room, and the green carpet where I sat listening to the librarian's voice, the scratchy green carpet where I rubbed my palms.

MY GRANDMA SAYS:

When your mom asked me and Grandpa to go to Canada, I didn't want to go. I said, I don't know English. But your mom said if we didn't go, she wouldn't go. So we went with her to Canada.

So boring! Back then, there was no Chinese TV yet. I bought a Chinese newspaper every day and read it from morning until night, even all the ads. Seven P.M., it was dark. On the street, there was no one, not even a ghost. Back in Hong Kong, I played mahjong with my friends every day.

Your grandpa and I didn't immigrate at first. We went on a six-month tourist visa. So we returned to Hong Kong after six months.

When I came back to Hong Kong, I couldn't stop crying. I cried every day. I didn't want to eat. I refused to drink water.

Then my mahjong friend invited me to go to Beijing for a seven-day tour. That was my first time going to Beijing. We saw the Great Wall, we walked along some of it. We ate fried dough sticks and Peking duck. That's when I finally felt better.

After we found out your mom was pregnant with your sister, your grandpa moved to Vancouver for good. But I only immigrated after your sister was born. When I went to the hospital and saw them draw blood from your baby sister every day, I started crying again.

FAMILY PRAYER

My grandma said every family has its own prayer that's hard to recite.

In the evenings before we slept, my grandma plucked her string of black beads from our nightstand to pray. We prayed to Kwun Yam for my sister to be healthy. We prayed to Kwun Yam for my mom to be happy. Then I pressed my palms together harder as my grandma recited the Buddhist prayer she knew by heart. I didn't know the words, I couldn't follow along, but once in a while it sounded like Pineapple Sock.

In my heart I repeated it—pineapple sock pineapple sock— thinking of my sister.

MY KINDERGARTEN TEACHER CALLS

One day my kindergarten teacher called to say, Your daughter doesn't play with other children. While her classmates play dress-up and kitchen and house, your daughter stands in the corner all day, furrowing her brows, cradling a baby doll.

MY MOM SAYS:

The year after we moved to Canada, I gave birth to your little sister. She was born with a big blood tumor on her shoulder, and almost no platelets.

The cancer doctor at the Children's Hospital took her case to conferences in the US and Europe because they didn't know how to cure her. One week before your sister's first birthday, they decided to give her steroids again. But after a few days on the steroids, she started crying a lot, and all of a sudden her moods were very strange. The blood from her tumor ran purple down her arm, so I brought her back to the hospital. The doctor decided to stop the steroids, but it took a whole week, because the dosage had to be halved and halved and halved again. He said that the only solution left was to try a new medicine from France, but no child had ever tried this medicine before, so they didn't know the side effects. Your dad and I decided not to do it. We told the doctor we wanted to try Chinese medicine instead.

Back then there was a little boy from Hong Kong who lived in Toronto, who was very sick. There was a campaign asking Chinese people around the world to Save Little Boy and donate bone marrow, and it was published in all the magazines in Hong Kong.

The Chinese doctor who eventually cured Little Boy became famous. Someone in our family, maybe your uncle, read about it and said to me, A doctor in Toronto healed Little Boy. Why don't you try to ask him?

I called my friend who lived in Toronto, and she helped me find the doctor's contact information and sent it to me. At the top of the form, it said that the doctor will treat good-hearted people, but will not treat bad-hearted people. It also said that the doctor never sees patients in person. All communication is through the fax machine, and payment is by donation.

You had to sign the form with your Chinese name, and if the patient was a child, then the parent had to sign it. Based on the signature, the doctor decided if you were good-hearted or not. So I faxed my signature to the doctor, along with a handwritten description of your sister's condition. Not long after, maybe a week, the doctor faxed back a prescription. He didn't write anything else. So I went to

Chinatown to buy the herbs and boiled them according to the instructions.

The instructions said that the Chinese herbs could not be boiled in a metal pot. I had to boil them in a ceramic pot, which was the only way the herbs wouldn't change in quality. The first time, I boiled the herbs in water until it was reduced to half a porcelain bowl of liquid. I poured this into a bowl and immediately boiled the herbs a second time until it was again reduced to half a porcelain bowl of liquid. Then I mixed the liquid from the first time with the liquid from the second time. I fed your sister right away with half of this mixture, which was two porcelain spoons, and put the other half in the fridge to heat up again later.

After your sister drank the herbs for one week, I wrote an update on her condition and faxed it to the doctor, and then he faxed back a new prescription.

A month after taking the herbs, your sister's platelet count rose from five to twenty, and the western doctor at the hospital said, Amazing!

At the next appointment, your sister's platelet count rose from twenty to forty, and the western doctor at the hospital said, So amazing!

Your sister recovered fully when she was two and a half.

One time, at the herbal shop in Chinatown, the shopkeeper looked down at the prescription, then looked up and asked, Is this from that famous doctor in Toronto? Is this for an adult?

I said, Yes, it's from that doctor in Toronto, but no, it's for a baby.

Then he told me that someone else walked in the other day with a similar prescription for an adult patient.

So, I don't understand. If an adult with a different illness was prescribed the same medicine, how did it cure your baby sister?

My friend said, Maybe the doctor healed her through the fax!

THE BROWN SLUDGE

I remember standing in the living room, and it was nighttime as they fed my sister the medicine.

My grandma clutched my sister's arms with one hand and held down my sister's legs with the other. My mom pinched my sister's nose, and tipped a porcelain spoonful of thick brown sludge into her baby mouth. Then my sister sprayed it all over the beige walls with a pucker.

AFTERNOON SNACKS

Since my mom was always at the hospital, my grandpa
took me to and from school, but it was my grandma who
made the afternoon snacks. Sometimes she peeled and
sliced juicy crystal pears. Sometimes she twirled a
chopstick in maltose syrup and glazed it on saltine
crackers. Sometimes she sizzled pot stickers, the warmth
of toasted sesame oil filling the house. But my favorite
snack of all was her sticky rice roll. In the middle of the
rice roll, cocooned by brittle seaweed and sweet fluffy pork
floss, crushed Lay's potato chips crunched in every bite.

When I was a kid, I didn't even have rice to eat. Every day I stood with my grandmother in long lines just to buy a few ounces of broken rice from the Japanese army. Broken rice bits, not even grains! We ground the bits into powder with a thick wooden stick, and boiled the powder in water. Like eating warm glue. Then we ran out of money, and my grandmother went away to dig trenches for Japanese soldiers in exchange for twenty-two pounds of broken rice.

After that, I lived alone. I was twelve or thirteen. My mother was a nanny, I don't know where. She rented a room for me on Gaoshing Street, in an apartment they separated into many rooms. One of my neighbors saw I had nothing to do, so she gave me all the classic books, like *Journey to the West, Water Margin,* and *Dream of the Red Chamber.* I'd only gone to school for one year, but I taught myself to read because I was so clever. My favorite book of all was *Romance of the Three Kingdoms,* which I read over and over. Sometimes we couldn't turn the lights on after sunset or we would get bombed, so on those nights I lit a long stick of fir sap—thicker than incense but thinner than a pencil—and held it close to the page. I read all night, I loved reading. By the time the sky got bright, the soot made my nose all black!

One time, I went to meet my mother and she gave me a bag of hot pork buns. As I walked home, the beggars along the street stared at me with their big eyes and sunken faces. Four of them started chasing me, so I threw them the buns and ran home. Everyone was so hungry then. On Goldfish Alley, I saw corpses with flesh cut out from their thighs.

Another time, I saw a man walking along the street smoking. At the end of the street, some Japanese soldiers told him to bow down in front of them. They made him eat the entire pack of cigarettes while pointing their guns at his head.

Then my mom didn't have money to rent my room anymore, so she took me to Macau, where I was born, to look for my father. He was the lead detective of the police department in Macau, and his office was right behind the Sing Ping Theatre. What I remember best is going to see Cantonese operas with my father. Back then the leading actress was plump and beautiful, and she wore a jade bangle so precious she covered it with a silk handkerchief before she walked on the street. My father and I went to the theater in the evenings, and if we were lucky, we found seats in the back. But I didn't live at his house, I stayed with a family friend. I should have figured out why.

I remember, one night I ran to his office, I burst through the doors shouting, Ba Ba, take me to the theater! Who knew there would be a woman sitting next to him. My father's coworkers said, Pour some tea for your new ma. I didn't understand, so I poured her a cup of tea and I called her Ma. Everyone laughed at me. That's when I found out my father had a new wife and lots of other children. But soon after, my father was being investigated for taking bribes, so my mother came and took me back to Hong Kong.

Miles away, my grandmother dug dirt all day and slept in the trenches at night. The earth was so damp it made her skin red and itchy. Her supervisor let her go, so she begged her way back to Hong Kong, but she couldn't find me because the building I'd lived in before was bombed. While she was begging on the street one day, she recognized an old neighbor who knew where I was, so that's how she found me again.

After that, my grandmother and I took a small boat to a rural village in Shenzhen, where my great-grandmother lived. She was one hundred years old and lived alone in a house the size of a bathroom. We slept on the ground next to her little bed. Every morning when we went to get firewood, my grandmother would cut down the big fir branches and I would cut down the little fir branches, ha!

The food in this village was the most delicious I've ever tasted in my life. Sometimes, my grandmother and I walked barefoot on the beaches and stuck our hands into the water to feel for clams and small stone snails. We pulled the meat out of the shells and boiled it in congee. It made the congee so fresh and sweet. On lucky days, we ate crispy rice sheets with salty marinated squid that we dried in the sun. But most days we ate tree bark and bits of yams left in the dirt. We were there for a year, I think. The people in the village wanted to marry me into a big family descended from generals in Qing dynasty. They wanted to sell me as a tungyeungsik—to marry me into the boy's family while I was still a child so that I would grow up in their house working as a servant, and when I was old enough, give birth to his children. Of course I didn't want that. Luckily, the war ended, so I followed my grandmother back to Hong Kong.

None of my children know these things. I've never told them, and they've never asked me.

PARKING LOTS

My grandma said I was clever like her because I was also born in the seventh month of the lunar calendar, when the gates of hell open and ghosts roam free. But my mom thinks the two of us need to be more careful.

One time, after we ate dim sum with our family friends in Richmond, my grandma carried me in her arms as we walked down into the parking lot. Halfway down the flight of stairs, she tripped and fell and rolled into the lane. A car screeched to a stop and ran its tire down my grandma's hair.

My mom was scared, seeing her mother and daughter lying there, scared that my little fingers were crushed. She once heard that spirits like to linger inside parking lots and at busy intersections, waiting for someone to take away. She says my grandma had curved her entire head and body around me, to protect me, and that if I hadn't been there, my grandma's arms would have flung out, her neck would have been straighter, so it would have been not her hair but her head under that tire.

My grandma says that day it felt like she was pushed by something—there was no way she would fall like that on her own.

That's why, to this day, she likes to say it was I who saved her life.

A story we love to tell in my family is that after my sister recovered, she followed me everywhere, and whenever I sat down, she pinched me.

On a typical afternoon, my sister, a toddler, chased me around the dinner table, and I, five years older, with tiny blue bruises on my arms, ran screaming.

But why didn't you just pinch her back? People would ask at this point of the story. Why did you let her?

Thing is, I would say, one day she suddenly stopped.

I stayed on guard for a long time, ready to run at any moment. But month after month passed, and she never pinched me again. She still followed me everywhere, jolly. But all she did now was copy my clothes and make me laugh.

MONKEYS

My sister and I loved sounds. We loved the way Cantonese sounds, like when our mom said bing ling baang laang when things fall and crash, and when she said ding ding instead of the tram.

When we heard a sound we liked, we echoed it through the house, and in our free time, we invented a laughing chant.

wahaha wabaHahahahaha!
wehehe webeHehehehehe!
wohoho woboHohohohoho!
wuhuhu wubuHuhuhuhuhu!

We laugh-chanted from morning to night, and then, when it was time to sleep, we clambered up the stairs like monkeys.

STARRY NIGHT

On weekends my mom drove us to art classes, even on Saturday mornings, even to the other side of town, even in the middle of winter when the streets were covered in snow.

In my very first memory of painting, the teacher held up a laminated print of Van Gogh's *Starry Night.* She scattered orange and yellow oil pastels across the table, and taught us to press curving dashes into the paper to make stars. We swirled deep blue watercolor and swept it over the dashes. As the blue water settled around the edges of the orange and yellow marks, I gasped, watching the stars emerge against the night sky.

At home, I practiced painting starry nights, while my sister drew fat multicolor cats. The floor rippled with paints and pastels. The walls danced with our art.

People often asked me, Do you come from a family of artists?

And I would say, There are no other artists in my family.

Only recently did I think to ask my mom, Why did you take us to so many art classes when we were kids?

My mom said she had always wanted to draw, but didn't know how to do it well. She thought if my sister and I learned how to draw, then we would be able to draw whatever we wanted.

She said, Lik bat chung sam—do you know what it means? It means, what your heart wants but you cannot do. It is an uncomfortable feeling. It's the feeling of wanting to do something and not being able to.

When I was a kid, I was always alone. Your grandma and grandpa worked all the time, your uncles had their own friends, and your aunts were two peas in a pod. I was the youngest and no one paid me attention.

At school, I was a lump of rice. The teacher's words went in my left ear and went out my right ear. But when the school wanted me to stay back and repeat the grade, your grandma found me a new school, and it was at this school that I started playing basketball. I joined a group that practiced every day after school, and by grade nine, I was on the school team. Did you know I was known throughout my school?

One time, it was almost the finals. We were practicing at school, and one of my teammates accidentally rammed into my left thumb. She started crying because I was in the starting lineup, I was one of the strongest players. As soon as practice was over, the coach took me to the bonesetter, where they wrapped my thumb over and over.

At the finals a few days later, my left hand was still in a large wrap, so when the game started, the coach told me to stay on the bench. All my teammates were worried because they were missing a strong player, and as the first half ended, our team was losing.

So the coach sent me out in the second half. Once I stepped on the court, everyone's morale went up, and my teammates became more steady. I didn't think about my thumb, I just played. Luckily, our opponents were fair and didn't bump into my left hand. Then I got two free throws, and each free throw had two shots. The first time, I scored both shots, and the second time, I scored one of the two shots. I was quite an accurate shooter then. In the end, we beat the other team by one point. That's how we won first place at the championship.

The game was on a public court, and lots of friends and classmates came to watch and support our team. That's how I got my nickname. After we won, my classmates shouted: One Hand Hero! One Hand Hero!

I remember best that your grandpa ordered fresh milk for us, two glass bottles every day. I poured myself a big glass of fresh milk when I got home after the game.

We were living in a public housing estate in Wang Tau Hom at the time. We were lucky because we got one of the biggest apartments on our floor, which was shaped like an H, with the big apartments at each of the four corners. Our apartment had a kitchen, so we plugged a plastic hose into the kitchen tap and took cold showers there. There was a drain in the kitchen floor, so we would pee there and flush it with water.

Otherwise, we had to go to the bathrooms by the stairwell in the middle of the H. There were men's and women's bathrooms, but there were no doors, just open cubicles. After you walked in, you didn't know where to step because the kids pooped all over the floor, and sometimes bad men would peek inside. I can't seem to let go of this part of the past. Even now, those bathrooms give me nightmares.

A SEPIA PHOTOGRAPH

My grandma said that even though their apartment was one of the biggest in the H-shaped building, there was only one bedroom. She and my grandpa slept in the living room behind a curtain, and put bunk beds in the bedroom for the other seven.

There were nine of you? I asked.

There was me and your grandpa, she said. Your mom, your five aunts and uncles, and my mother.

Your mother? What was she like?

Not good. But she was very beautiful.

Do you have any pictures?

My grandma shuffled into her room and came back out with a sepia photograph, torn at the edges and creased all over. In the photograph, two young women with wispy bangs, wearing plain dresses with high collars, stand in front of a painted landscape, facing the camera. My grandma pointed to the tall one with the piercing gaze.

Back then, she said, many Chinese men were sold like piglets to the West, to build railroads and to work on farms. My great-grandfather was sold as an indentured servant to a fruit farm in Tahiti. In Tahiti, the farm owner's daughter fell in love with him and followed him back to China. She eventually learned to speak the local dialect, but the villagers called her gwaipo for the rest of her life. That's why my mother was so beautiful—she was the granddaughter of a Tahitian beauty. She was so beautiful, and she gave birth to me, so ugly. Maybe I look like my father.

I have a square face and a big mouth. One of my eyes
has a monolid and the other has a double lid. But at least
I'm pretty clever, right? Did you know I was the one who
got us the big apartment in the first place? Before that,
all nine of us lived in a single room in the Jordan
neighborhood. Outside our building, there was a medical
van, with a doctor we could go see. One day, I went
downstairs to the van to see the doctor. Coincidentally,
the nurse was not working that day. I said, Why isn't there
anyone here to take names? The doctor said, Well, do you
want to do it?

The pay was one hundred and forty dollars, including
cleaning the van. The van was a bit bigger than a seven-
person van. Inside, there was a desk and a long chair for
patients to sit. It was really easy to clean the van and to sign
people in. The doctor saw that my handwriting was nice, so
he hired me.

Soon after, a talented female doctor started working in the van. She'd just moved to Hong Kong from the mainland and couldn't work in a hospital yet. She taught me how to give an injection. You break the needle at the top and then you flick the needle. You poke the butt cheek one-third of the distance from where the bone is. She said, I'll let you practice on my fat butt!

It's easy to put a needle in a fat butt. But then someone came in to get a shot, and it was an old person, whose butt was very wrinkly. It was so hard to put the needle in.

Then there was a different nurse who prepared the medicine. One time, that nurse went out to lunch and told me to prepare the medicine for her. Back then, I didn't even know the twenty-six letters of the alphabet. An old lady came in to pick up her prescription. The doctor had decreased her dosage from one pill to half a pill, but I didn't see clearly what the doctor wrote, so I gave her one of everything. Afterward, when I looked at the prescription again, I started sweating and sweating. After that, I was more careful.

One day, the area official came in to get a hormone shot. While I was poking the needle into his butt, I thought to say,

There are nine of us in my family living in only one small room, and I want to apply for a better one. I don't know how, but he helped me apply for that apartment in Wang Tau Hom, the one your mother just told you about.

How come I remember the past so clearly? These days I walk into the kitchen and forget what I wanted to eat!

LUNAR NEW YEAR

Every year when my dad came to Vancouver for Lunar New Year, our house had to be clean and quiet. For two weeks, everyone tiptoed up and down the stairs, and watched television with the volume on low.

Before every meal, my sister and I had to address each adult at the table, starting with our dad. We couldn't watch Cantonese detective dramas or talk with food in our mouths, so we ate in silence, only the clink-clink of chopsticks against our porcelain bowls.

Gwaai, my mom would say. Be gwaai for these two weeks. Your dad works so hard for you in Hong Kong.

But the real reason we were quiet was because my dad was jet-lagged, and whenever he couldn't sleep, he got angry, his eyes reddening behind his wire-rimmed glasses. He never raised his voice though. His anger was the cold clenched kind that left the room in silence.

My mom says that for a few years after we immigrated to Canada, every time my dad left for the airport, I cried. But I don't remember that. When I think of Lunar New Year growing up, I think of the black lacquer box my mom filled with salty watermelon seeds, candied lotus root, and milky White Rabbit candies. I think of sitting cross-legged on the carpet with my sister and laying out our red pocket money. And I think of counting down the days until our house could be itself again.

SUMMERS

Everyone says Vancouver is best in the summertime—not too hot, not too cool, not a drop of rain. But we were never there to enjoy it because as soon as school got out, my mom, my sister, and I packed our suitcases and flew to Hong Kong.

Everyone says Hong Kong is worst in the summertime. It's so hot you sweat as soon as you step out of the shower, so humid that it's hard to breathe. And on top of that, summer is typhoon season, so it's often pouring rain.

THINGS STRANGERS IN HONG KONG
SAID TO ME EVERY SUMMER

Are you back for summer holiday?

As soon as I saw you, I could tell.

Where are you back from?

My friend's niece is also in Canada, but she's in Toronto, very cold.

You speak Cantonese better than she does though.

Will you come back to Hong Kong to look for jobs when you're older?

You should come back, or you'll grow roots over there.

How did I know you grew up abroad?

I can tell from your innocent face!

LUCKY BAMBOO AND MONEY TREES

At some point in high school, my dad moved into a new apartment in Hong Kong. Unlike the old one, the new apartment was clean and bright. It had a balcony that looked out on the sea. In the living room, a beige couch faced the television, and a second couch sat perpendicular. Ten dark wood chairs surrounded a long dining table, with my dad's chair at the head. In the corners and along the walls, lucky bamboo grew in clear water vases that glinted in the sun, while braided money trees rose from white and blue porcelain pots. My dad beamed as he gave us a tour of his new home.

During the day, when my dad was at work, my mom, my sister, and I walked around the malls, soaking in air-conditioning. Sometimes we went to lunch with our aunts, and sometimes we went to see the herbalist. In the evenings, while my dad watched the news, my sister and I bent over our laptops, chatting online with our friends. We spent the whole summer this way, and then, at the end of August, we flew back to Vancouver, carrying suitcases of clothes still damp with humidity.

YELLOW TULIPS

When I was in grade eleven, my grandpa felt a sharp pain
in his jaw, and when my mom shined a flashlight into his
wide open mouth, she saw a ball of pink flesh growing
inside.

After my grandpa checked into the hospital, my dad
and all my aunts and uncles came from Hong Kong to
Vancouver to see him. My mom said I didn't have to visit
him since I was nearing finals and it was important that I
study hard.

And when my grandpa died, everyone attended the funeral,
everyone except me because I had an exam that day. I
remember that night after they came home from the
funeral, I sat on the couch watching a Cantonese comedy,
maybe with an aunt or two. I remember laughing extra
loud, I wanted to hear my own laughter, I wanted it to
travel through the house.

My dad told me it was vulgar of me to be so loud at such a time. He said, Who knows what your relatives are thinking of you now.

The day my grandpa died, he converted to Christianity. As he lay in the hospital bed, he turned to my mom and asked her to call the nuns. I don't know how my mom knew these nuns. When the nuns arrived, they stood on each side of him, and said prayers as they held his hands. Then my grandpa closed his eyes.

They say the funeral was joyous. My mom said she had never been to a funeral like it before. The nuns sang prayers, and the room shone with light. My sister said at one point everyone stood in a circle and sang to celebrate his life.

When my mom thinks of her father, she thinks of how he rushed back to Vancouver as soon as he found out my mom was pregnant with my sister. She thinks of all the steamed buns he kneaded with his hands because she was so hungry then. And she thinks of a Cantonese saying: Trees want to be still, but the wind won't stop blowing. When children want to care for their parents, it's already too late.

When I think of my grandpa, I think of the jolly old man who befriended all our neighbors in Vancouver, who made the juiciest pork and vegetable dumplings, and who planted yellow tulips in our backyard in the spring. I think of his bright face, wishing me good morning, every single morning, with the enthusiasm of a child.

THE PAINTING OF HORSES

In my last year of high school, my mom asked me to make a painting for my dad. The Feng Shui master advised my dad to hang one in his apartment, on the wall behind his chair at the head of the dinner table.

The painting has to have nine horses, my mom told me. They have to be galloping.

I went to the art store and picked out sturdy stretchers and thick cotton canvas. I bought a new set of Windsor & Newton oil paints and different sizes of soft sable brushes. I bought a brush cleaner jar with a metal coil inside, and a new can of odorless mineral spirits. I searched online for an image of nine horses galloping, but I couldn't find one, so I took an image of six horses galloping and an image of three horses galloping from the same perspective, and photoshopped them together. Then I painted the canvas with a ground of yellow ochre, sketched the outlines of the horses with burnt sienna, and blocked out the dark areas with raw umber.

When I started hearing back from colleges, I stopped painting. I couldn't sleep at night. My hair fell out when I touched it. I didn't look in the mirror because every day my face grew a new pimple.

In the end, I was accepted to two colleges. Deciding between the two, I called my dad to ask for his advice.

It's up to you, he said. Both are good, but neither one is Harvard.

When my mom saw me slouched over my desk that night, she said, Choi yung sat ma—do you know what it means? It's a proverb about an old man who was sad because he lost his horse. But it was a good thing in the end.

Why was it a good thing?

I don't remember, but the point of the proverb is, what you think is bad might be good, and what you think is good might be bad. Choi yung sat ma, that's what it means.

I spent the months after that studying for my provincial exams, driving around with my friends, and packing my suitcases. Then I left for college.

Four months later, when I came home for winter break, my mom asked me when I was going to finish the painting.

I don't know, I said. I don't make realistic paintings anymore.

So my dad went to a painting factory in Shenzhen and hired a painter there to make one for him.

In the painting, nine horses gallop through a lush forest clearing, their manes gilded orange by the rising sun. My dad hung the painting in his apartment, behind his chair at the head of the dinner table, in a three-inch carved golden frame.

THE GAME

The first time I flew to Hong Kong by myself was the summer after my first year of college. My sister was still in high school, so my mom stayed in Vancouver with her. I'd applied to ten internships and gotten one at an advertising agency in Hong Kong. It was the first time my dad and I would spend a full month together without my mom and sister.

It was the summer of 2006, which meant it was the World Cup. I knew my dad liked the Brazil team, so I asked if he wanted to watch their match together after my first day at work. I called to let him know I was heading home from the office. It seemed like something a good daughter would do.

Hello? he said.

I'm coming back now, I said.

Who are you talking to?

I'm talking to you?

When I got home, he was sitting on the beige couch, staring ahead through his wire-rimmed glasses. The television was off.

Why didn't you address me? he said, still staring at the blank television.

What are you talking about?

When you called, why didn't you say, Hi Dad?

Are you serious? I called to tell you I was coming back.

I lay down on the couch perpendicular to him and stared at the ceiling.

Look at me when I'm talking to you, he said.

I counted the ridges in the pale yellow lamp above me.

Look at me, he said.

Why are you making such a big deal out of this? I said.

He stood up and walked out of the room, slamming the door.

I went to my room, took out my laptop, and crawled into bed. Half an hour later, I heard a quiet knocking. I got out of bed and stood there, facing the closed door.

The World Cup is starting in a few minutes, my dad said.

I imagined him standing on the other side of the door, facing me. Maybe he would be looking at his feet.

I don't feel like watching it anymore, I said.

I listened to his footsteps padding away.

I got back into bed and watched the game from my laptop, not leaving my room until the next morning.

MY HARD HEAD

My mom says I had a hard head even before I was born.
She says it's because she drank herbs throughout her
pregnancy, prescribed to her by a miracle herbalist in Hong
Kong. So that when she was in labor in the birthing ward,
and the doctor sucked me out with a vacuum, all the
nurses gasped at how round my head was, how the skull
was already formed.

That's why you're so stubborn, my mom says. And you
inherited your dad's bad temper too. But at least your head
isn't pointy.

SIR

That summer, I got to meet my dad's college friends. There were six of them, including my dad, the entire class in the Department of Business Management that year. My dad picked a nice buffet restaurant so that everyone could eat as much as they wanted.

So what was my dad like in college? I asked, as soon as we sat down with our food.

Everyone respected him.

He was president of this, president of that.

Student council.

Volleyball team.

A good student.

A good person.

Our nickname for him was Sir.

I looked over at my dad, who was sitting at the other end of the table, laughing as his classmate patted him on the shoulder.

The night before, as I was walking toward the front door of our apartment, I saw his one place setting at the long dinner table. There was a white porcelain bowl on a white porcelain plate, a pair of wooden chopsticks, and a white porcelain spoon.

I thought then of my mom, my sister, and me, in Vancouver, sitting around the dinner table eating pizza pockets and giggling on a Saturday night. My mom would say, Your dad must be awake by now, give him a call later. And I hoped she would forget, or my dad would be in the bathroom when we called, or lightning would strike the telephone lines across the street. What was I supposed to say to my dad, if I didn't have any new accomplishments to tell him? And why did I always have to do all the talking?

I looked back at his place setting on the table. I saw, in one moment, all the other times it sat there. With the news on, while a typhoon lashed rain against the windows, as a fly buzzed around the room. During the green spring, through the humid summer, in the white morning light of winter. For most of the year, he worked all day, came home to eat alone, and couldn't fall asleep at night.

I turned the doorknob and shouted, Dad, I'm going out to meet my friends now!

Okay, enjoy! he said, from somewhere in the kitchen.

As I descended in the elevator, face-to-face with my reflection, I counted all the seconds it took to reach the ground.

MY MOTHER CALLS FROM CANADA
WHILE I'M IN HONG KONG

I talked to your dad on the phone the other day, my mom said. He couldn't sleep. He said he was regretful.

Of what? I asked.

He regrets that we raised you and your sister in Canada, while he worked so much in Hong Kong.

Why?

He said you don't have Chinese roots. He said a Chinese person should know the Chinese language, culture, and history, but you and your sister don't. He said you don't even know to address him when you call.

Are you serious? Then why did we move away in the first place?

Because we didn't know what was going to happen after '97.

Then why didn't we move back to Hong Kong like everyone else?

When you and your sister were kids, I asked if you wanted to move back, and you both wanted to stay.

MY MOM SAYS:

I asked you two if you wanted to move back to Hong Kong the year your sister was in grade three. That spring, cherry blossoms bloomed everywhere in Vancouver, and your sister was allergic to cherry blossom pollen. She couldn't fall asleep, even though she tried sleeping in every room in the house, including my closet. Eventually she started missing school. I asked your sister if she wanted to move back to Hong Kong, where there weren't so many flowers everywhere, but she refused. You were already in grade eight then, so you didn't want to move back either.

Of course, it's better to be together as a family. Taking care of everything alone was hard. All I had was the telephone. Every Sunday, I waited for your dad to call. Many of my friends took their kids back to Hong Kong after getting their Canadian passports, not caring if the kids were happy or not. It was called Wui Lau—the tide returns, the water flows back to Hong Kong. No more flying here, flying there. Families were happy together again.

But I thought if both of you didn't want to go back, then I wouldn't force you. I would go back by myself after you went to college, and by then, where you lived would be up to you.

PAJAMAS

I remember, after we immigrated to Canada, sneaking into my parents' bathroom once. My dad had just left for Hong Kong again. The black bathroom tiles were cold on the soles of my feet. I reached down into the white plastic laundry basket, and pulled out his faded striped pajamas. I buried my nose in them, so I could remember what he smelled like until he came back.

Though I grew up studying western art techniques, when I got to college, I wanted to learn Chinese ink painting. I applied to study abroad at the China Academy of Art in my junior year.

In Hangzhou, I stayed at the international student dormitory. My room had a glass table for a desk, a dark wood chair, and a dark wood bed. On the bed was a hard mattress. My window looked out on a teal basketball court, encircled by a brown four-hundred-meter running track. In the evenings, when there was a basketball game, they turned on the stadium lighting. On these nights, I opened the curtains to let the fluorescent light flood my room against the black sky.

My dormitory was across the street from the West Lake. Along the lake walking path, pale green weeping willows bowed down to graze the water. Smooth stone bridges led to pagodas with curved eaves. Sometimes, to the staticky sound of erhu from a plastic radio, groups of old people practiced tai chi together, moving slowly as one body.

In the mornings, I attended class with six other international students. Our semester was divided into three parts: Copy of Bird-and-Flower Works, Copy of Landscape Works, and Calligraphy. Like the local students, who were far more skilled than we were, but who had a much harder time enrolling at the China Academy of Art, we learned by imitating old master works every day.

We stood around our teacher's desk as he showed us how to paint ink bamboo. After wetting the brush with water, he dipped it in black ink and smoothed the tip across the rim of the inkstone. Hovering the brush above the bottom edge of the raw mulberry paper, he painted each gray bamboo segment with a quick upward stroke.

This freehand style of painting, the teacher said, is called xieyi. Xie is to write. And yi is idea or meaning. To write meaning, what does that mean? Unlike the painters of the royal court, who layered multiple colors and outlined the finest details, the artists who invented xieyi painting were scholar-amateurs, and they were not interested in depicting the physical likeness of things. They left large areas of the paper blank because they felt empty space was as important as form, that absence was as important as presence. So what did they seek to capture instead? The artist's spirit.

The teacher looked at each of us, nodding, before dipping the brush in more ink. Then he dashed a thin black line across each node of bamboo. The black lines bled out into the damp gray stalks, alive.

Watch the way I am sitting, the teacher said. Good posture is important because it allows your qi to circulate through your body, to flow into the brush and breathe into the artwork.

He painted each leaf with a single stroke.

When you look at a good xieyi painting, the teacher said, you feel the artist's spirit. Look at this hanging scroll of lotus. Look at this sketch of shrimps. How fresh, how spontaneous. Almost childlike, don't you agree? With a single line, you can paint the ocean.

BAMBOO GROVES IN MIST AND RAIN

After class, I walked to a teahouse by the West Lake. A layer of mist hovered above the water, and among the dangling weeping willows, peach blossoms began to bloom. I sat down by the window and ordered osmanthus tea, which I had never tried before. In the glass teapot, hundreds of tiny yellow flowers floated in hot water. I lifted the lid and the steam smelled of apricots and honey.

As I sipped the tea, I searched for Chinese women artists on my laptop, and began reading about the poet and painter Guan Daosheng. Born in 1262, she was considered to be the greatest female painter in Chinese history, known for her paintings of ink bamboo, which was an unusual genre for women artists at the time. Bamboo was thought to embody strong and gentlemanly qualities—the ability to stay green through the winter, and to bend without breaking. Guan's bamboo paintings were widely praised. Critics said her confident and vigorous brushstrokes showed no signs that they came from a woman.

My research on Guan Daosheng led me to another artist, active around 925, known as Lady Li. In one account, Lady Li sat outside one evening and noticed the swaying shadows of bamboo under the moonlight. In a moment of inspiration, she picked up her brush, dipped it in ink, and traced the shadows on her paper window pane. From then on, more and more artists imitated Lady Li's technique, and that was how the genre of ink bamboo was born.

Guan was married to the artist and calligrapher Zhao Mengfu. In her husband's studio, nine years before her death, she wrote an inscription on one of her paintings:

> To play with brush and ink is a masculine sort of thing to do, yet I made this painting. Wouldn't someone say that I have transgressed? How despicable, how despicable.

This inscription survived, but the painting itself is now lost. Even though Guan Daosheng was seen as the greatest female painter in all of Chinese history, she has only one authenticated painting surviving today. Titled *Bamboo Groves in Mist and Rain,* the beautiful paper scroll shows feathery groves of bamboo growing along the edge of a riverbank. This artwork is an example of Guan's lasting contribution to the genre: she took the technique of ink bamboo and integrated it into landscape painting.

Out of curiosity, I looked up how many of Zhao Mengfu's paintings remain. It turns out there are countless. His works are collected around the world.

A month later, my dad came to Hangzhou. I suggested he visit during the hundredth anniversary of the China Academy of Art, since there would be celebrations. The night before he arrived, I couldn't sleep. I realized he had never visited me anywhere before, and we hadn't spent any time alone since I interned in Hong Kong two summers back. I read every tourist guide to Hangzhou, and made a spreadsheet of itineraries.

It was sunny the day my dad arrived. We watched the opening ceremony, which began with firecrackers and a lion dance. Several famous artists attended, and many of them signed the school guestbook with beautiful calligraphy. We stared as an old man with long gray hair and a long gray beard dressed in long gray clothes signed the guestbook. We listened to a woman play pipa in the lobby.

Then I gave my dad a tour of the school campus, and led him to the international student exhibition. For weeks, I

crumpled painting after painting before submitting one to
the jury. Unlike oil painting, ink painting was unforgiving,
and I couldn't cover up mistakes with more paint.
Whenever I hesitated, holding the brush still for a second
too long, the ink flooded the delicate paper. I didn't tell my
dad that my painting had been accepted. I wanted it to be a
surprise.

We walked up the pale wood stairs to the top floor. The
room was bright, and on the white wall across from the
stairs, my painting hung in a dark wood frame under a track
of lights.

In the painting, I am riding a brown bird. We are soaring
above tree after tree, and each one is white and translucent.
I washed white watercolor on gray rice paper to create that
effect.

I titled the painting *Ghost Forest*.

My dad stood in front of the painting for a long time,
holding his hands behind his back.

Without looking at me he said, I think there is something
wrong with you that you're making art like this.

I stood there and watched as he walked away, still holding his hands behind his back. As he paced through the rest of the gallery, I stayed a few steps behind him.

Afterward, we went to Lingyin Temple, a Buddhist monastery. The word Lingyin translates to the place where one's soul retreats. Founded in 326, it is one of the largest Buddhist temples in China, with numerous halls, statues, and grottoes within.

At the entrance, framed by deep green foliage, peaceful gray rock reliefs of Buddhas watched over the long line of people waiting to go inside. They say the temple is famous because people who pray there often see their wishes come true. We walked around in silence, entering the halls together, kneeling before different statues of Buddhas, putting our palms together to pray.

When we took a taxi back to the city center, I asked my dad what he wanted to do next.

Shouldn't you be the one taking me around? he said.

We could go to the flower garden, I said.

Would that be your top recommendation?

I don't know, I haven't been there yet.

You've been in Hangzhou for over a month. You're not very ambitious, are you?

I watched the West Lake pass by outside the taxi window. Mist began to collect on the glass, and soon, tadpoles of rain raced across the windows.

My ankle hurts, I said. I don't feel like walking anymore.

I asked the taxi driver to drop me off at my dormitory instead. When we arrived, I got out of the car and went up the stairs without looking back. I walked down the dim hallway and knocked on my classmate's door. She was cooking tomato soup on a hot plate in her bathroom.

I thought you were showing your dad around, she said.

Can I have some? I said, staring at the bubbles on the surface of the soup.

I sat down on her bed and ate two bowls.

THIS BEACH WOULD BE PERFECT

I remember going on a rare family vacation once, a few years before my dad died. We were walking along the beach, my dad, my sister, and I. The sand was white and so fine. We waded in, the water licking our shoulders cold.

This beach would be perfect, my dad said, if the rocks weren't so sharp on the soles of our feet.

I looked down through the water, and lifted my toes. We swam in small circles. Then, as we dried ourselves on the sand, my dad squinted at me.

You'd look better if your face were thinner, he said. And if you were two inches taller.

GRINDING THE INK STICK

After my dad returned to Hong Kong, the days in
Hangzhou got warmer and the tulips by the West Lake
bloomed. My classmates and I completed the Copy of Bird-
and-Flower Works part of our semester. As a treat, our
teacher took us on a field trip to his studio outside the city.

Our taxis slowed down to a stop at the edge of a golden
field. In the middle of the field stood a small white house
with thin stalks of purple bamboo growing along its walls.
We walked through the field toward the house and stood in
front of the entrance. Among the purple bamboo, white
butterflies fluttered.

The teacher led us into the house and up the stairs. As we
sat down at a large wooden table, his assistant lit a stick of
incense and steeped green dragonwell tea leaves that were
handpicked before the yearly rains. The teacher took out an
ink stick and an inkstone, and laid a fresh sheet of mulberry
paper on a thick piece of cream felt. Adding a bit of water,

he ground the ink stick against the inkstone in clockwise circles. It made a soft scratching sound.

Looking up he said to us, I am not simply grinding the ink. When I grind this ink stick, I am clearing my mind. I am preparing for the painting. Sometimes I sit here, just grinding the ink for half an hour, making space in my mind.

For my final project at the China Academy of Art, I wrote a piece of calligraphy. Using black ink on mulberry paper, I wrote three simple characters in bold clerical script, and mounted it on silk.

心如水

Heart like water

I wrote it, thinking of my grandma, who only went to school for one year, but who knows more Chinese characters than anyone in our family.

It's such a shame, my mom likes to say. Your grandma is so intelligent. She would be famous, if only she were born decades later, instead of in 1930.

My aunt has a theory that my grandma hasn't yet fulfilled her life's potential, that she hasn't accomplished what she came into this world to do.

I think about some of the things my grandma has done—read classic historical novels, written an opera, starred in that opera, and distilled that opera in the style of Tang poetry.

MY GRANDMA SAYS:

It was by chance that I wrote my own opera. I was living in Guangzhou at the time, and there was a government campaign to get women out of the kitchen, so I started working at a ceramics company. At the company, some people made money selling the bowls and plates, and some people did the accounting. All of them were men. Women were only allowed to stick flower paper on the bowls and fire them in the kiln.

When the Hundred Flowers Campaign started, the manager told us to organize some cultural activities. I found out that the men in accounting and sales knew how to play the gongs and drums. Doong! Doong! Chaang! Those things. One of them even knew how to play the erhu. One of your aunts is learning how to play the erhu now, and it sounds like she is carving a chicken.

I'd seen many Cantonese operas with my father during the time I lived in Macau, and I'd read the *Three Hundred Tang*

Poems during my one year of school. Because in Tang poetry, the last characters of the first, second, and fourth lines have to rhyme. Every line except the third. So I knew how to do it.

Ming ming ming ming. Like that.
Wah wah wah wah. Rhyming.

And I was very intelligent, ha! I wrote the entire opera in four and a half hours. It was a one-act Cantonese opera called 仙女會鋼帥, *Fairy Meets Steel Commander.*

In the opera, people collect all the steel in the country and melt it. The sparks fly so high they disturb the gods in heaven. A fairy descends to earth to see what they are doing. When she meets the handsome steel commander, they begin dancing together. The government reviewed my opera, said the theme was correct, and approved it for performance.

At the show, I played the lead actress. I was the fairy that came down to earth, and my tall broad-shouldered female colleague was the handsome commander. We rehearsed together at work, and then we went to a nearby shop to borrow costumes. On the night of the show, I brought all my children to watch. All my children except your mom, she wasn't born yet. One of your aunts overheard someone in the audience say I looked like a star.

The audience stood up and clapped for a long time. I bowed and walked off the stage to a room in the back. Inside the room, I saw a big table with brush and ink, and a poem came to me. Do you want to hear my poem?

鋼鐵火花衝上天
驚動天上眾神仙
引來仙女會鋼帥
雙雙飛舞在人前

Steel sparks surge up into the skies
The gods are disturbed and surprised
Descending fairy and captain meet
Together they dance before our eyes

I wrote out the characters in big strokes across the cloth, and later, when the company manager walked into the room he said, Who wrote this poem? The calligraphy is beautiful.

All my colleagues pointed to me and said, She did! She did!

The manager asked, Did you study literature in school?

I said, No, I only went to school for grade three!

THE LIVER AND THE SPLEEN

There is a Cantonese saying my dad liked—I think he wrote it himself. He said: Before age forty, we use our health to make money. But after age forty, money can't buy back our health.

My dad was sixty-one when he started getting sick. At the time, I was living in London, where I found a job in advertising after graduating from college. My mom called me one night to say she bought a one-way ticket to Hong Kong because my dad was in the hospital, his feet and belly were swollen, and he had liver disease.

I don't understand, I said. Dad doesn't even drink.

According to traditional Chinese medicine, my mom said, the liver restores itself between eleven P.M. and three A.M. You know your dad, he hasn't slept well in years. Having a bad temper and working too much are also bad for the liver. But don't worry about him! Worrying is bad for your spleen.

WOULD IT BE SO DIFFERENT?

For a time in elementary school, whenever I closed my eyes at night, I saw my parents dying. I saw their faces smiling at me. Then I saw them lying in the hospital, in a scene from a Cantonese drama, and everything was blinding white. What would I do, how would I survive? I reminded myself that I saw my dad only twice a year. Would it be so different? Then I pulled the blanket over my head so that all I could see was black.

THE SCRIPT

After my mom called to tell me that my dad was in the hospital, I decided to take time off work. I knew my parents would tell me that there was no need to fly all the way from London to Hong Kong, that my work was important, and that I shouldn't worry. But when I imagined my dad in a hospital gown, feet and belly swollen, all I could think was that I never visited my grandpa before he died.

When I talked to my boss, he said, Take some time off and go tell your dad you love him.

I realized I'd never told my dad that before. No one ever said it in my family. I decided to call my childhood friends, the ones I grew up with in Vancouver.

Have you ever said I love you to your parents? I asked. Have you ever said it in Chinese?

No! they said. Why would we?

But for the rest of the day I thought, What if I never had the chance?

After I got home from work, I sat down on my couch and looked out the window. A streetlight flickered as a red double-decker bus hissed to a stop below. I waited for my dad to pick up, shifting my phone from hand to hand so I could wipe the sweat off from my palms.

When my dad answered, I told him I was going to visit, I'd already requested the time off work, and would be flying to Hong Kong in two weeks. Then I talked about the weekend, and then I talked about the rain.

Finally, he said he was tired and needed to rest.

Wait! I said. I love you.

Thank you! he said. I could hear him smiling.

Two weeks later, I boarded my flight to Hong Kong. The first night I arrived, I sat at the dining table while he watched the news. I went to the kitchen and poured myself a glass of water and drank it, and then I poured another one. As I waited for my mom to take a shower, I pretended to watch the news with my dad. Finally, he stood up, got into his bed, and turned off the light. His door was ajar, so I poked my head in.

I love you, I said.

There was no answer. I didn't know if he was asleep. I walked back to my room and plopped facedown on my bed.

Days later, my dad's belly began to bloat again, so we went to the hospital. I had used up all my vacation days and had to fly back to London that night. A few of my aunts and uncles came to check on my dad, and they were standing around the hospital bed. I didn't want to say it in front of them. But as I was about to leave for the airport, I turned to my dad one more time.

I love you, I said.

He looked back at me, eyes blank.

A month later, I called him and said, Every time I said I love you, I was kind of disappointed you didn't say anything back.

You're getting a lot of western education, my dad said. We're Chinese. It's not important for us to express our feelings. Underneath this sky, all parents love their children.

I thought, I should let this go. He told me that all parents love their children, what more do I want?

Then I thought, no, I want to hear it. So I decided to come up with a script.

THE SCRIPT

Hi Dad,

Happy Father's Day! (Coincidentally it was Father's Day the next day)

我爱你! (I would say I love you in Cantonese, even though it would sound extremely weird because nobody ever said it in Chinese, not even in television dramas)

Do you love me?

Can you tell me? (In case he replied with only Yes to the last question)

I rehearsed the script in my head all next day at work, and called him in the evening.

Hi Dad, I said.

Hi, he said.

Happy Father's Day!

Thank you!

我爱你.

I love you too! he said in English.

Thank you! I said, hanging up right away.

The next day I woke up laughing.

MOTHERS

All those western people, my mom said over the phone, they use the word love for everything. They say it like they say hello.

When I didn't answer, she kept talking.

She said, I know you're upset at me, but that's how it is, I get upset at your grandma too. And your grandma got upset at her mother all the time. Maybe it runs in our family.

MY MOM SAYS:

She was beautiful, your great-grandmother, when she was young. Nose a little high, eyes a little big.

But she drank this stuff. I had to buy it for her once. You had to go to a special pharmacy and say, I want to buy cough syrup, and they would give it to you from a room hidden in the back. I don't know what it was, I was only a child then, but it wasn't alcohol. It was clear, and she drank it from the plastic bottle. She was always drinking from that bottle.

We lived together in the same apartment for many years, the one where you also lived when you were small. One time, she went out to play mahjong with her friends and forgot her keys. She called someone, who called someone, who called me. I was at the office, I had so much work to do, so I took my time getting home. She was sitting in the lobby, shaking. That's when I realized she needed her bottle.

I was at the office when she died. Only one of your aunts was at the hospital to watch her go. At the time, your grandma was in a different hospital because she'd just had surgery. She was so angry none of us told her that her mother had died.

But she'd just had surgery, what else were we supposed to do?

FIFTEEN

My grandma told me her mother arranged for her to meet my grandpa when she was only fifteen. He was twelve years older, tall and thin, with slicked back hair and tinted half-rim glasses, a tailor. They watched a few movies and had a few dinners.

What did you think of Grandpa the first time you saw him? I asked.

Nothing, my grandma said. I didn't think any thoughts.

Did you want to marry him?

I was only a child. I did what my mother told me, so I would have food to eat.

What was it like when you got married?

We never got married. Your grandpa came to Hong Kong when he was nineteen to escape a marriage, but when his father was dying, he went back to his hometown and his family arranged a wedding for him. When I met him, he had left behind a wife and children in Shanghai. I was seventeen the first time I gave birth. I had all six of my children by the time I was thirty.

MY GRANDMA SAYS:

Your mother was my last birth. I was living in Guangzhou at the time, taking care of your five aunts and uncles, while your grandpa worked in Hong Kong. When the veins were big and my belly was big, the doctor said, If you have another one after this, your veins will burst. He said, Don't have any more!

I insisted on getting my tubes tied right after I was going to give birth. The doctor said, Aren't you afraid that this is dangerous? Who's going to sign your papers? So I got my grandmother to sign the papers.

Coincidentally, it was 1959, the Soviet Union and China had a bad relationship, and they forced China to pay its debts. Hospitals didn't have the usual supplies and medications. They injected half a cc of anesthesia into my belly, and opened it with a knife.

Above me: a big bright light. Half a cc of anesthesia. I could see in the reflection what the doctor was doing.

It wasn't that painful, but it was so, so sour. The doctor hooked the tube out and tied it, while teaching two students. The doctor hooked the left one out, then hooked the right one out, then tied both ends.

It was so, so sour. Sweat like I went swimming. Since that day, I can't stop sweating.

Years later, after we had moved to Hong Kong and I was in my fifties, I was menstruating and it lasted nine days. Usually, it was only three days. It wasn't a lot of blood, and it was very thin. But I went to the Queen Elizabeth Hospital and told the doctor. Actually, it was menopause, but I didn't know it at the time. I didn't have cancer or tumors or anything.

Still, the doctor said, Let's remove it then!

They cut out my uterus and removed my fallopian tubes too.

After the surgery, you're supposed to take hormones every day until you die. But after taking it once or twice, my throat felt a bit sore, so I stopped. I'd heard that taking hormones could cause breast cancer. So I didn't take them, haven't taken them since.

That's why I'm always sweating. Sometimes I sweat just from drinking a cup of hot tea. When I go out to buy groceries, I put a towel on my back, and it gets completely wet. I have to go home and change my clothes. After I change, I start sweating again.

FRESH TOWELS

Wherever my grandma goes, she carries extra towels and plastic bags in her purse. In the bathrooms of malls and restaurants, she lifts up the back of her shirt, removes the soaked towel, and folds it into a plastic bag. Then she shakes out a fresh towel, tucks the edges under her bra straps, and smooths her shirt back down.

SLEEPING PILLS

The doctor prescribed half a sleeping pill to your dad, my mom said over the phone.

He didn't take it, right? I said.

Your dad was the one who asked for it. He told the doctor that he hasn't been able to sleep. He asked the doctor to help him.

But Dad hasn't been able to sleep for years. I thought he was against sleeping pills.

I thought so too.

So he's been taking them for the last two months?

No. After taking half a pill, he would sleep for only two hours and wake up again, so he wanted the doctor to prescribe the whole pill after a few days. Soon, he started to say things that didn't make any sense. The nurse said maybe his liver couldn't metabolize it. One night, when he asked me to give him the sleeping pill, I told him I already gave it to him. He fell asleep soon after.

Then what happened?

I started giving him a foot massage whenever he woke up because every time I give him a foot massage, he falls asleep right away.

What happens when he wakes up in the middle of the night?

I give him a foot massage every night from eleven P.M. to two A.M. because that's when the liver renews itself. After that, I go to sleep.

You give him a three-hour foot massage every night?

What else can I do? I think the nurses started suspecting something because the other day, the doctor asked me if the sleeping pills were working.

What did you tell him?

I told the doctor that your dad was sleeping fine without them because I was giving him a foot massage every night. Then one night, in the middle of the night, a nurse came into the room. I think the doctor sent her to see if I was telling the truth. Luckily I really was giving your dad a foot massage at the time.

Mom, I can't believe you've been giving Dad three-hour foot massages every night! You have to take care of your own health too!

Don't worry. It's not like I'll be doing this forever. After he gets better, I'll have plenty of time to rest.

A SIMPLE LIFE

A week later, I flew to Hong Kong too. When I landed at the airport, the sky was white. I took a taxi from the airport straight to the hospital, and found my dad awake in his bed.

After I recover, my dad said, I'm going to retire. I want to take your mom on vacations.

Where will you go? I asked.

I want to go everywhere. I won't be picky about it.

Where would you want to go first?

Maybe Greece. And when I get better, I want to live a simple life. And I want to try pizza.

POPEYE

We used to play a game called Popeye, my dad and I. We stood at opposite ends of the room, facing each other, the length of the beige carpet between us. Then we ran toward each other and wrestled. I think he was Popeye because he picked me up and swung me around and poured invisible cans of spinach into his mouth. I laughed so hard my feet kicked the air. I don't know what the point was, but it was my favorite game.

SO HANDSOME

My dad asked my uncle to give him a haircut and a shave.

So my uncle arrived at the hospital with a pair of scissors and a razor. We sat my dad up on a chair and draped a few white towels around his shoulders.

My dad, who had always been clean-shaven, now had wiry hairs, a third of an inch long, growing here and there on his chin. His hair was greasy and matted in the back. His skin had a yellow tinge.

My uncle trimmed the hair at the nape of my dad's neck. He leaned in close and he squinted his eyes and leaned back to trim some more.

When he was done, we peeled off the towels from my dad's shoulders and swept away the stray hairs.

Doesn't he look handsome? my mom said to the nurse who just walked into the room.

So handsome! the nurse said.

My dad smiled, showing his teeth.

It was the happiest I had seen him in days.

HAIR

For as long as I could remember, my dad took good care of his hair. He combed it every morning and evening, massaged hair growth oil on his scalp after showering, and used the blow-dryer in small circles. Whenever he walked into an elevator, or past a shiny window, he checked his profile and patted the spot at the back of his head where his hair always stood up.

One day, while sitting near his bed in the hospital, I asked if he wanted me to clean his hair.

No, it's okay, he said.

Are you sure? Maybe it'll help you sleep, I said.

Okay, then.

I took out the coconut oil, which my mom had decanted into a glass dispenser bottle. I pumped two pumps into my palm and squeezed myself into the space behind the hospital bed. I lifted his glasses off with one hand, and warmed the oil in my palms. I noticed that the whites of his eyes were pale yellow. I placed my thumbs together at the top of his forehead and pressed gently down to his temples. I continued doing this along the middle of his scalp. Then I pressed my fingers in small circles behind his ears. After a while, I filled a small bowl with hot water, dipped cotton pads into it, and smoothed them across his head to wipe off the oil. His scalp was pale and clumps of his hair came off onto the cotton. I took out the blow-dryer and dried his hair, moving the dryer around so it wouldn't get too hot. Then I took out his wooden comb and parted his hair, combing it down on each side several times.

THREE WOMEN

There are three women I owe in my life, my dad said. They are my mother, my older sister, and your mother.

Why do you owe them? I said. I sat next to his hospital bed.

They have all been so good to me. And I've had such a bad temper.

A lot of people have bad tempers though.

No, he said. When I was a kid, I was really skinny. I'd get cold at night and wouldn't be able to fall asleep. I shared a bed with my sister, and she could always tell when I was cold. So she would wrap her big thighs around me until I was warm and fell asleep. The thing is, she's deaf and mute. She's deaf and mute!

He shook his head and looked away.

THE FISH

My dad said he learned his first big lesson when he was six years old.

He said, I was really good at fishing. Out of our nine siblings, I was the best. One day, my sixth brother asked me to bring home a big fish for dinner. I said, no problem. I even invited the fat twins next door to come with me. I wanted them to see me catch the fish.

We walked down to the docks. Not long after, one of the twins pulled a big fish out of the water. I watched it plop down right next to me. There were no more fish after that.

I went home and told my sixth brother.

It's okay, he said. Now I know never to rely on you again.

That was my first big lesson.

VACATION TIME

I stayed at my dad's apartment while my mom spent every night at the hospital. Finally my aunt insisted on watching over my dad for a few nights so that my mom could rest at home.

One night, my aunt woke up to my dad shouting.

Wake up! my dad said.

What's going on? my aunt said.

We're all leaving now. Pack your bags!

What? Where are we going?

We're going on a cruise!

HAPPY MOVIES

Dad must be so bored, I said to my mom one evening before I left the hospital. Maybe I can bring a movie on my laptop tomorrow.

Make sure you pick a happy movie, my mom said. You know how your dad is, he won't be able to fall asleep if it's sad or scary. He still brings up that time years ago when your cousin was staying with us. In the middle of the night, your dad was thirsty and went downstairs to get a glass of water, and as he turned the corner, your cousin emerged from the bathroom with a white head band in his hair and a white moisturizing mask on his face. Your dad didn't sleep for days.

MY FATHER'S FATHER

One day, I realized I didn't know anything about my dad's father. I'd never even seen a picture of him. My dad was sitting by the hospital window, eyes closed, in a chair inside a square of yellow sunlight.

What was your dad like? I said.

He wasn't home much, my dad said.

What did he do?

He was an artist. He was very talented. The paintings he made looked like photographs, and he took photographs too. He wrote beautiful calligraphy. But he liked to drink, and when he drank, he had a bad temper. Once in a while he would come home for dinner and have a few drinks.

That must have been hard for you, not having him around.

We didn't have time to think about those things back then.

MORNING

When I arrived at the hospital the next morning, my dad was wide awake in his bed, staring ahead through his wire-rimmed glasses. My mom had fallen asleep in the chair beside him.

Do you want to listen to some music? I asked.

Okay, he said.

I scrolled through my phone and clicked on an album.

This is by a jazz musician called Thelonious Monk, I said.

I turned on the little speaker next to his pillow.

This album is called *Thelonious Alone in San Francisco*, I said.

A while later, poking out from under the blanket, my dad's feet wagged from side to side. He still stared out the window with no expression.

Outside, rain fell soft as mist.

I closed my eyes, imagining each piano note as a fruit-flavored hard candy, drifting out of the speaker and floating around the room—cherry red, apple green, berry blue, and lemon yellow—dancing, hovering, from time to time flashing in the sun, and falling, falling to the ground one after another, clinking here and there in the bright light of the morning.

MOM, SAY IT!

My sister finished her exams at college and took the next flight to Hong Kong.

As soon as she arrived and the nurses stepped out of the room, my dad motioned me and my sister over to the right side of his bed.

You two, come stand here, he said.

He motioned my mom over to the left. And you, come stand here.

He reached over to his bedside table and lifted his wire-rimmed glasses with his thumb and forefinger. He put on his glasses and stared at the wall.

Then he turned to me and my sister.

I love you, he said to me.

I love you, he said to my sister.

My sister and I looked at each other before turning back to him.

We love you too! we said.

Then he faced my mom.

I love you, he said.

My sister and I swiveled to our mom, eyes wide.

She stood there, looking at her feet. Then she started giggling.

Mom! I said.

Mom, say it! my sister said.

We stared at her as she kept giggling.

Then she said, I just farted!

Later, my mom, my sister, and I walked to a restaurant near the hospital for lunch.

While waiting to cross the street, I turned to my mom and asked, Was that the first time Dad ever told you he loved you?

As the light turned green and my mom walked on, I thought I saw her smiling.

THE STORY OF HOW MY PARENTS MET

My sister and I have tried, many times over the years, to find out how our parents ended up together. Once, my sister spent the entire day poised like a T. rex, index fingers pointing forward, as she followed our mom around and poked her in the back, chanting, Tell us! Why won't you tell us! Even then, all we got was a shrug and a smile.

What I know is that after my mom graduated from high school, she worked as a bookkeeper at a stationery company for two years. When she decided to find a new job with a higher salary, she brought home a newspaper, combed through the listings, and mailed out letters to apply. The first company that wrote back was the office where my dad worked.

MY MOM SAYS:

I wasn't supposed to have any children, you know. When I was twenty-one, my right lung collapsed. The first doctor I saw said I needed surgery, but the second doctor I saw said I needed injections. I decided to get the injections, so every night after work, I went from my office in Kwun Tong to the doctor's clinic in Central. Luckily, the subway in Hong Kong was built by then.

All the nurses had different techniques. The good nurses got the shot on the first try. But some nurses took so many tries. One time, one particular nurse couldn't get the shot inside my elbows, so she moved to the back of my hand. I felt a pain like an electric shock, so she stopped right away. Another nurse told me that the last nurse had bad eyesight. Back then, I didn't know to speak up. Back then, I could have said, I don't want this nurse to do my injection. In the end, I got a lot more than twenty-five shots. I was so relieved when it was over.

But a year later, my left lung collapsed. I was at the office when I felt a loud pop in my left side. Every time I took a breath, I felt the air clawing down inside me. When I stood up, it wasn't as painful, but the moment I lay down on my bed, the air was like a big wind blowing paper cuts inside my windpipes. And I don't know why, I couldn't stop coughing. So I had to go back to the clinic, and get the injections all over again.

After my lungs collapsed three times—right, then left, then right—the doctor said to me, If you get married in the future, don't have any children. It's too dangerous if you get pregnant and your lung suddenly ruptures. If you really must have a baby, then you have to get a C-section. And at most, you can have one baby only.

By the time my lungs collapsed for the fourth time, that doctor had immigrated to Australia, so I found a new lung specialist, who looked at the X-ray and prescribed me some medicine.

I asked, What about the injections?

He said, Injections? There are no injections for this. Just take the medicine, and you'll be fine.

I took the medicine and recovered. I thought, Why did I get all those injections before?

Then one night, at a big family dinner, your aunt told me about a miracle herbalist who had just come to Hong Kong from the mainland. When I went to see this herbalist, I asked him if it was true that I couldn't have children because of my lung condition. He said, That won't be a problem after you take these herbs!

Around this time, your dad told me he wasn't feeling well. Every day around two o'clock at the office, he felt very tired and unable to move. I convinced him to go see the herbalist with me. After checking your dad's pulse, the herbalist said, Around two o'clock every day you feel very tired. It's because your liver has swollen by an eighth of an inch.

We went back to see the herbalist every Sunday. We got married one year later.

Actually, in 1985, I went to see a fortune teller, the one who named you after you were born. He was very famous at the time. He said, Your current boyfriend is such a good boy. Doesn't smoke, doesn't drink, doesn't gamble. I can tell by the shape of your nose.

He asked me if I had another boyfriend before. I said yes. He said, Good, because if not, then you will break up. But since you've had a breakup already, then this is the right one. Next year is the right year. Next year, get married.

He said, You have three daughters and two sons in your life. Whether you want to give birth to all of them is up to you.

We sat in the hospital room, reading emails on the hospital's Wi-Fi, my mom, my sister, and I. My dad lay in his bed.

What do you need? my mom said. Do you need something?

I looked up and saw my dad fumbling his hand around the space beside his pillow.

Do you want me to call the nurses? my mom said.

He kept pawing at the net of tubes and cords, until he grasped a black rectangular box and pushed the red button with his thumb.

A minute later, a nurse walked in and asked how he was doing.

He met her eyes for a second and looked back at the wall ahead.

What would you like? the nurse asked.

I looked at my mom to see if she knew what was happening.

Then a second nurse walked into the room.

What's going on? she said.

I don't know, the first nurse said.

Did he poo?

Did you poo?

You did, didn't you?

I think he did.

Let's see.

The two nurses stepped forward and pulled the pale green curtains all the way around the bed, clinking the silver curtain hooks.

Let's see what's going on, one of them said.

From where I sat, through the thin wavering crack between the curtains, I saw my dad close his eyes as they turned him on his side and pulled down his pants.

FAVORITE COLOR

My mom asked me and my sister to watch over my dad while she went home to take a shower. My sister and I sat on each side of the hospital bed, resting our chins in our hands and our elbows on the railings.

Dad, I have a quiz for you, I said. The first question is, if you could choose only one, would you rather get a compliment or a hug?

I'm not interested in this quiz, my dad said. He closed his eyes and pretended to sleep.

Dad, what's your favorite color? my sister asked a few minutes later.

Brown, my dad said, eyes still closed.

My sister and I looked at each other, eyebrows raised.

Later my sister said, Who says their favorite color is brown?

THE SPANISH RESTAURANT

I have a proposal, my dad said. But I don't know if you'll be open to it or not.

What is it? I asked.

Raise me up first, he said.

He likes the bed at seventy degrees, my mom said.

I looked around at all the buttons near the bed.

What? How do I know if the bed is at seventy degrees?

You have to use the level app on your phone, she said.

I found the level app on my phone and raised his bed to seventy degrees.

How's this?

Good, he said. I heard there is a famous Spanish restaurant not far from this hospital. It's expensive and celebrities go there. I want you to take your mom and your sister there for dinner tonight.

I'll call and make a reservation.

No, I don't want you to make a reservation.

Why? It'll be easier if I call in advance.

No, I want to see if you'll manage to get a table.

What do you mean?

It depends on how confident you act. You might have to speak to them in English.

He turned to my mom.

I want to test her marketing skills, he said, chuckling.

I looked at him, then at my mom, then back at him again. Was he serious? I looked at his hair, sticking out in all directions. Then I followed the thin tube of oxygen curving into a loop before running up into his nostrils, and the pale yellow albumin on a drip. What was wrong with him? Was he delirious? Why in the world would he want to test me now? I wanted to walk out of the room.

She's only here for a few more nights, my mom said. Why don't we go to the Spanish restaurant another time?

SOMETHING TO TALK ABOUT

The day before I flew back to London, my dad said: There's something I want to talk to you about.

What is it? my mom asked.

No, not you, you can't listen. Go do something else, he said. He motioned for me to sit next to him.

I sat down next to the hospital bed.

I've been thinking about this for a very long time, he said. And I just don't understand.

What is it? I asked.

I looked at his hands clasped together, papery yellow skin on bones.

You've been this way since you were a child, he said. You seem cheerful when you see me, but I can see in your eyes that it's not real. When you ask me questions, I can hear you're not really asking me questions. I keep wondering, what have I done wrong?

FATHERS

I asked my grandma if she saw her father again after the war.

She said, The last time I saw my father was in 1962. Through a friend of a friend of a friend, he found my address in Hong Kong.

What did you talk about?

Nothing. We talked about nothing, and then I never saw him again. Sometimes I wonder if he's gone yet. Well, I'll be ninety soon.

ICU

There was a waiting list for livers in Hong Kong, so the doctor advised my dad to transfer to a hospital in Hangzhou, where he could get a transplant sooner. My parents flew to Hangzhou a few months later, and I booked my flights to meet them there.

My dad became unconscious shortly after and was put in the ICU. They said that maybe it was from the pressure of flying.

The visiting hours in the ICU were only between two and three o'clock in the afternoon. I was relieved. This was the only way my mom would rest at night.

In the taxi, from the airport to the hotel, I left the window open so I could feel the rush of the wind on the highway. The sky was thick and gray, and roses streaked bright pink along the roads. I hadn't been back since my semester of studying here. I would have never guessed that six years later I would return to see my dad in the local hospital.

I arrived at the hospital fifteen minutes early, and waited with my mom outside the doors to the ICU. There were several other families waiting. As soon as it turned two o'clock, a nurse unlocked the doors and poked her head out, and we all rushed toward her. We stood in the entryway, a group of families, putting on plastic gowns, plastic caps, plastic gloves, and plastic shoe covers. All of the plastic was baby blue.

I walked with my mom toward the room directly across from the entrance.

My dad lay on the bed near the window. There was a nurse standing next to him, writing on a clipboard. The other bed was empty and untouched. I wondered when they changed the sheets on it.

My dad had been unconscious for days. His body was thinner than I remembered, and curled into a fetal position.

Say, I'm here, Dad, my mom said.

I'm here, Dad, I said.

You have to say it louder so he can hear you. My mom leaned in close to his face.

We're here now, she said. We're here! Give us a sign! If you can hear us, give us a sign!

I stood there, nodding and patting his hand.

Call your dad back, my mom said. You have to call him back, loudly.

We're here, Dad! I said. We're here!

Did you hear that? my mom said. We're here!

We took turns leaning in and shouting, but as soon as the nurse walked out of the room, my mom glanced at the door. Then she pulled a small glass spray bottle out of her pocket.

This is from the temple, she said

She sprayed the water in the room a few times, in all different directions, muttering something, then sprayed it on a cotton ball, and dabbed that onto my dad's forehead.

This is from the temple, she whispered.

I waited for my dad to wake up.

Then, it was three o'clock.

Later, my mom and I walked to a restaurant by the West
Lake for dinner. My mom didn't want to look at the menu,
so I ordered us clear fish soup, steamed silken tofu, and a big
pot of osmanthus tea to share. While we waited for the food,
my mom stared out the window at the weeping willows,
not saying a word. I asked her what was wrong.

I made a mistake, she said.

What happened? I asked.

I spoke to the Feng Shui master, and he said that we aren't
supposed to call your dad back while he is unconscious. We
aren't supposed to shout at him. I did it so many times. And
we aren't supposed to do that.

It's okay, I said. You didn't know.

She shook her head and closed her eyes.

The next day, the nurses informed us that my dad regained consciousness. My mom and I entered the ICU with my sister and uncle, who had arrived in the morning. We all put on our baby blue puffy outfits, and followed the nurse down a different corridor. My dad lay there—the room shone with sunlight—his eyes darted among our faces. His lips were stretched around a ventilator, and he turned his head from side to side.

It looked like he wanted to say something, so I wrote out all the letters of the alphabet on a piece of paper and told him to blink when I pointed to the letter he wanted. After two letters, he shook his head and kicked his feet. He started to write Chinese characters with his index finger on the bed. My mom and uncle tried to guess the characters, but they couldn't figure out what he was trying to say. I told him to write English letters so that I could help.

In a circle around the bed, we all bent over my dad's index finger, as he wrote letters on the mattress, one by one.

He wrote the first letter.

W ?

He shook his head.

N ?

He shook his head again.

L ?

He kept writing with his finger on the bed.

Finally, we guessed M.

Now he closed his eyes slowly, pausing.

It's M! The first letter is M! I said.

I felt like I had won a prize.

We leaned in again to watch his finger.

                                    O ?

No, it's not O.

                   U ?

U. I think it's U.

S ?

T ?

Must! My sister and I shouted. Must what, Dad? Must what?

He looked exhausted from the writing. It must have taken us ten minutes to get here, and we were only at the first word.

He kept writing.

The next letter took us a while, until we said G, and he closed his eyes slowly again.

Then, O.

GO? My sister and I looked at each other and burst into tears.

No, Dad, we said. Don't go! Please don't go. You're going to get better!

Where are you going, huh? my mom asked.

I didn't understand why she was so calm.

A

W

A

Y

My sister slumped over the railing on the other side of the hospital bed. Everything was cloudy through my tears.

My dad kept writing.

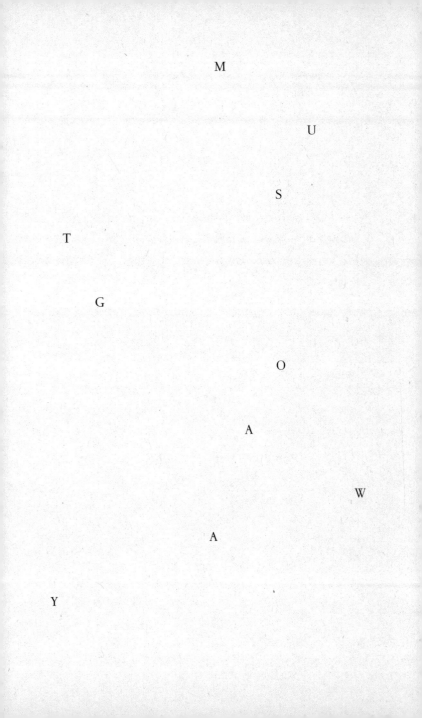

We still have so many vacations to take, my mom said. You promised me you would take me on vacations. You haven't taken me on any vacations yet.

He wrote it all over again, letter by letter.

Dad, don't go, please, my sister said. Please.

Don't give up, Dad, we said. Please don't go.

He shook his head from side to side and kicked his feet.

I WILL NOT GIVE UP

We clapped and cheered.

Yes, Dad, don't give up!

W

H

Y

Y

O

U

C

L

A

P

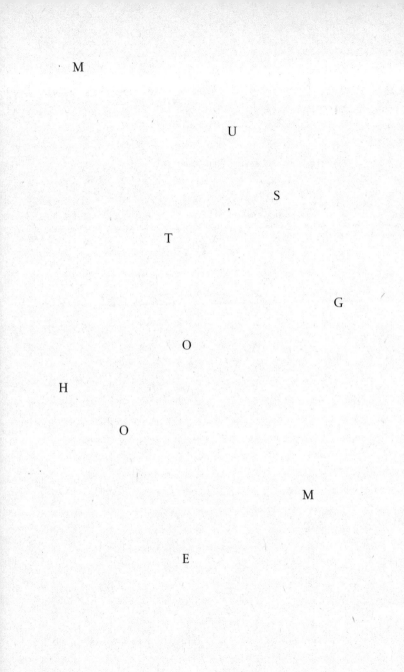

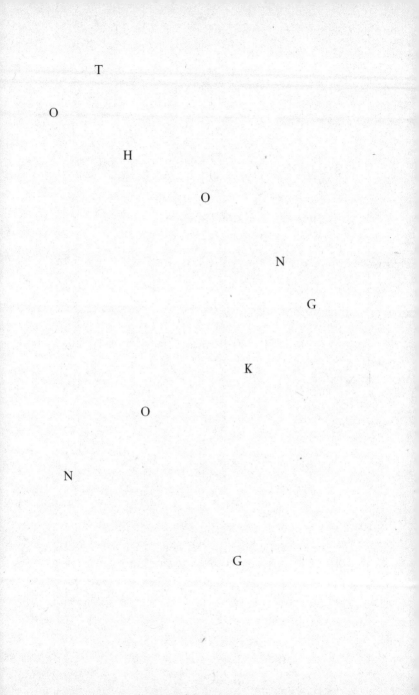

Wait, you want to go to Hong Kong?

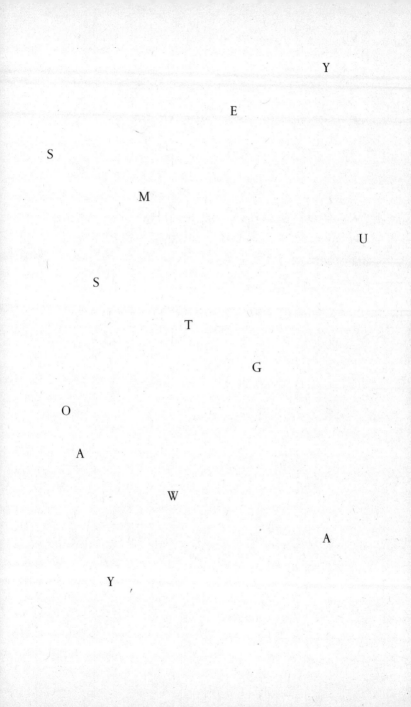

If you want to go to Hong Kong, you have to get better first, my mom said. We'll go back after you get better and get a transplant.

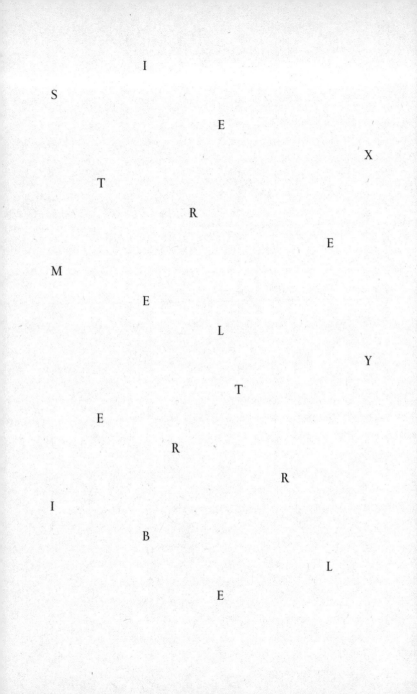

My sister and I looked at each other.

Why didn't he just write *bad*? my sister said.

We started to laugh and couldn't stop.

FOUR A.M.

That afternoon, when visiting hours were over, my mom told my dad she was going to rest and would return in the morning. My dad shook his head and kicked his feet. He glared at my mom and gripped his lips around the respirator. Since we noticed the family next door always stayed past the visiting hours, we asked them how they did it. They said if we were quiet, the nurses would pretend not to see us. So, my mom stayed overnight, sitting on a wooden stool by his side.

The next night, my sister and I stayed so that my mom could go take a shower and sleep on a bed. When my mom told my dad she was leaving, he shook his head from side to side until she was out of the room. My sister and I sat there in our baby blue plastic hair caps and gowns, on each side of the bed, staring at our feet.

It was summer in Hangzhou and there was no air-conditioning.

We sat in silence as the light inside the room faded from gray to gray-orange to gray-blue and shadows moved across our faces.

After it got completely dark outside, my sister looked at me, slowly tucking her face into a double chin and grinning. I checked the ceiling corners a few times in case there was a surveillance camera. Then I flared my nostrils and fluttered my fingers near my ears. We hid our faces below the plastic railing of the bed and emerged each time with a new facial invention. We performed grand dance gestures and mirrored one another. We put our arms around each other's shoulders and did lunges around the hospital bed.

I could see drops of condensation forming inside my shoe covers.

By four A.M., my sister was asleep on two rectangular wooden stools that she put back to back as a makeshift bed.

Once in a while, my dad woke up, eyes wide, and shook his head from side to side. My mom had said that when this happened, it was because the evil spirits were trying to take him away.

I sat next to him and took his hand, watching his face. Each time he woke up, eyes wide and shaking, I stood up over him and straightened my shoulders, inhaling, exhaling, looking steadily into his eyes and patting his hand.

Each time, when his eyes focused on me, his face softened, and he fell asleep again.

DONGPO PORK

One of my favorite things about Hangzhou is the food.

They have a dish called Dongpo pork, which is pork belly
that has been stewed in a thick sauce on low heat for hours.
It is so rich that it is served only as a two-by-two-inch
square, in a tiny brown clay cup, with a bit of sauce. The
layers of meat and fat alternate like a luscious cake, covered
by thick shiny translucent skin. They say that women
should eat the skin more often because it's full of collagen.
The dish is named after the poet Su Dongpo.

We ordered it several times while we stayed with my dad in
Hangzhou. Usually we ordered one and cut it into four
pieces to share. In my mouth, the fat melted and the meat
fell apart, oozing sauce. It was delicious. It left a layer of oil
shining in the brown cup.

THINGS MY DAD LIKED

- Steamed rock cod with sweet soy sauce
- Bright-colored clothing, but not on himself
- Boiling hot Cantonese double-boiled soup
- Hong Kong, his home
- Hair growth oil and wooden combs
- Converse shoes for his narrow feet
- The color brown
- The evening news
- Views of the sea
- Mr. Bean
- The World Cup, and the Brazilian soccer team
- *The Sound of Music,* his favorite movie
- Poached chicken with ginger scallion sauce
- Sunshine and hot temperatures
- Studying the Heart Sutra
- Sliced papaya on a plate
- Perfect handwriting
- Practicing tai chi
- Falling asleep

YELLOW

My mom persuaded the doctors at the hospital to let my dad have acupuncture once a day in conjunction with the western treatment. Because he had water swelling, after the acupuncturist pulled out each needle, yellow fluid surfaced. With gloved hands, my mom, my sister, and I bent over and dabbed the liquid away with soft cotton squares. By the time we finished one section, the liquid seeped out again.

A million tiny yellow domes shining all over my dad's body.

We're going back to Hong Kong tomorrow, my mom said. Pack all of your belongings.

After speaking with the doctors at the hospital in Hangzhou, my mom decided to take my dad back to Hong Kong. They expected it to be a long time before he would be healthy enough to get a transplant.

Since regaining consciousness, he asked over and over to return to Hong Kong, and every time my mom assured him that they would be going back soon, but not until he got the transplant. Every time my mom entered the hospital room, he glared at her.

Y O U A R E E V I L, he wrote with his index finger.

Eventually she gave in, with the doctor's permission, so we packed our bags and took the next flight to Hong Kong.

THE BIGGEST HURDLE

Back in Hong Kong my mom said, This morning your dad said Kwun Yam came to him last night. She told him that he overcame the biggest hurdle, and everything is going to get better from here.

I looked over at my dad. He was sleeping in the hospital bed. The green-gray blanket covering his body rose and fell as the ventilator gasped in and out. The air conditioner hummed. He was home now, in Hong Kong. Even the shape of the ventilator looked smaller, his face and lips more relaxed.

How did he tell you? I asked.

He wrote out the characters with his finger, my mom said.

Do you think it's true?

Kwun Yam is watching over your dad every day.

TEMPLE OF RED AND GOLD

That weekend we went to the temple to pray. We stood in a long line that led up to a man sitting at a small table covered with stacks of red and gold papers. In one hand, he held a pencil, and in the other, a cigarette. His teeth were yellow.

Above us, thick coils of incense burned in slow spirals. A woman knelt on the floor, shaking a cylinder of bamboo fortune-telling sticks with both hands, filling the air with the sound of maracas.

Everything inside the temple was red and gold.

When we got to the front of the line, my mom said: We're here to pray for my husband's recovery.

She handed the man with the yellow teeth some money, and he led us over to the big gold Buddha statues. He lit several sticks of incense and handed one each to my mom, my sister, and me. He started to chant, hitting a small gong, and from time to time, he told us to bow.

It was cold, and the air was thick with smoke. My nose started to run. I wiped my nose with the back of my hand. The man kept chanting, and we kept bowing. Every time I bowed my head, my nose ran more. I tried to make it look like I was scratching my nose. I thought, people are probably too busy to notice anyway. After a long time, the man said we were done. We thanked him and stepped out of the temple doors.

The sun was so bright. I lifted my hand to shield my eyes.

EMERGENCY SURGERY

Three days after we returned to Hong Kong, my dad had
to have emergency surgery, and we were not allowed to
visit him at the hospital until the afternoon.

That means we get to sleep in tomorrow, I said to my sister
the night before.

When we arrived at the hospital, my dad was asleep.

He's very tired from the surgery, the nurse said.

So my sister, my aunt, and I went out to buy snacks. We
bought matcha milk chocolate and airy pink shrimp chips
and pineapple juice boxes.

When we got back to the hospital, my dad was still sleeping.
My mom sat in a chair beside him. We waited for a few
hours, then we decided to go downstairs for dinner.

You should eat something, I said to my mom. Or get some fresh air outside. It's so stuffy here.

No, I'm okay, she said. You can bring something back for me.

My mom stayed in the hospital room with my dad the entire time.

We took the elevator down to the cafe in the basement of the hospital. We ordered clear winter melon broth and thick hot and sour soup, braised soy sauce noodles and mango tapioca pudding. We laughed and joked. We ordered Singapore fried vermicelli in a takeout box for my mom.

Mom should really loosen up and take care of her own health, I said to my aunt and my sister.

When we got back to the room, several of my aunts were standing at the foot of my dad's bed.

Why did you eat for so long? my mom said. The doctor says your dad won't live through the night.

What do you mean? I asked.

The nurses came to wipe his body, and after that, he became unconscious, my mom said. I've already notified our family and friends.

I walked over to my dad.

His eyes were wide open and pointed at the ceiling.

WAITING

We stood in a semicircle around the bed.

We have to decide if we'll save him or not, my mom said. Of course we'll save him.

The numbers on the screen were falling.

What do you mean save him? I asked.

It might break his rib cage, my mom said.

What did the doctor say?

The doctor said we shouldn't.

We stood there, looking.

Are we going to save him or not? my mom asked.

The doctor and nurses rushed into the room with the crash trolley.

They stood there, waiting.

Are we going to save him or not?

I don't know, Mom. I don't know!

HANDS, ONE

You've got to tell him happy things, one of my aunts had said, back when my dad first checked into the hospital. Hold his hand. Tell him that he has to walk you down the aisle one day. You've got to hold his hand and say these kinds of things.

Would I just reach out and put my hand on his hand? From above or from below, like a handshake? Should I hold his hand with both my hands? What if he won't want to walk me down the aisle?

When I landed in Hong Kong, I took a taxi from the airport straight to the hospital. I walked into the room, put on a surgical mask, and rubbed alcohol gel on my hands. As I walked over to my dad's bed, I saw his arms outstretched, his hands reaching for mine. His cheeks were hollow. I went over and took his hands in mine.

I'm sorry, he said.

I started to cry.

I love you, he said.

I love you too, I said.

I'm sorry for not being a good father. I'll try harder when I get better.

After that, I held my dad's hand every day.

WATCHING

We stood in a semicircle around the bed.

One of my aunts lunged forward.

Don't worry, I'll take care of my younger sister! she shouted.

I looked around at everyone else. Was I supposed to speak too? What was I supposed to say?

My mom stepped forward and, with her arms still by her side, she rested her cheek gently on my dad's chest.

It was the most affectionate gesture I had ever seen between them.

When she got up and stood back in the semicircle, I went and did the same.

HANDS, TWO

I was holding his hand, the day he died. It was smooth and bloated, like a glove filled taut with water. I looked at his face, then I looked up at the numbers on the screen. Then I looked at his face, and then I looked up at the numbers on the screen. I don't know why I looked at the numbers on the screen so much. After a while, I realized his hand was warm only where I held it. So I held onto his hand with both my hands, one hand to keep the thumb half warm and one hand to keep the pinky half warm. Then I moved one hand to his wrist because that was getting cold too. I kept moving my hands around, as evenly as I could. I can't remember how long I did that for.

Later, one of my aunts said, You've got to let go of his hand. Otherwise, his soul won't leave in peace.

So I let go of his hand then.

YOU CAN GO IN PEACE

We couldn't close his eyes.

One of my uncles said, It's me. I'm here now, you can go in peace.

One of my aunts said, He wasn't ready to go. That's why his eyes are open. There's something he wasn't ready to leave behind. Maybe you'll be able to do it. You try.

I stepped forward and lifted my right hand, lowering it slowly onto my dad's forehead. I felt his eyelids on the edge of my palm.

Don't worry, Dad, I said. You can go in peace now.

I imagined his eyelids slipping down under my hand. But they felt rubbery, like they had been glued onto his eyeballs. I lifted my hand and lowered it down again, pressing harder. I breathed in and out and tried one more time.

My aunt said to my sister, You try.

I held my breath. What if my sister could do it?

My sister tried to do the same.

His eyes were still wide open when they loaded him into the truck.

TAKE CARE OF YOUR MOTHER

Because my dad passed away within twenty-four hours of the surgery, the police had to investigate the death. As my dad lay motionless on the hospital bed, we gathered around the policemen outside the room.

We didn't want them to investigate the death. We didn't want to sue anyone. We just wanted a peaceful funeral with the body intact.

The policemen said we could pick up the body from the morgue the next morning.

After they left, we went back into the room to say goodbye one more time.

We don't want to let you go, my uncle said.

Some hospital staff came into the room and wheeled my dad out and into the side elevator. We followed them, taking the elevator down into the parking lot. We followed my dad's body as it was pushed toward a large truck. The light in the parking lot was fluorescent gray. We stood there, watching the men in dirty white T-shirts load him into the truck.

Say safe journey, my mom said.

Safe journey, my sister and I said.

We stood there for a while. As we turned around and walked toward the exit, some relatives came over to me.

You're the oldest daughter. Take care of your mother, one of them said.

Remember, you have to take care of your mother now, another said.

Be strong. Take good care of your mother for me, a third one said.

My uncle pulled up in his car and drove us home.

SINGAPORE NOODLES

When we walked in the door, the light in our apartment
was golden. I went into the kitchen and washed my hands
with three pumps of soap. The bubbles smelled like fresh
jasmine on my skin. Then I scraped the leftover Singapore
fried noodles into three bowls, and heated them in the
microwave. My sister went to shower.

As my mom and I sat there, eating the bright yellow
vermicelli, I saw a flicker on the balcony, on the other side
of the glass. My dad was standing there, waving at us,
smiling. I could tell that he was happy, and that it was the
first time in a long, long time. I smiled back.

The noodles are delicious, I said.

Delicious, my mom said.

THE PICTURE WE TOOK AT THE BEACH

We need a picture of your dad for the funeral, my mom said.

Does it have to be big? I asked.

I don't know, but find a nice one, she said. I don't have any recent pictures of him.

I opened up my laptop and scrolled through my photo albums. I didn't have many pictures of my dad either. Most of the ones I had, he wasn't smiling. After a while, I found one that I took of my parents when we went to Bintan Island three years earlier, just before he got sick. It was the first time we had traveled together as a family since I was a child. In the middle of the photograph is a pale tree trunk wrapped in thin rope. Patches of sunlight lie here and there on the sand. There are two blue and white striped reclining beach chairs on either side of the tree trunk. On the left side, my mom is leaning back and grinning. Her beach chair has sunk into the sand. On the right side, my dad is sitting up, his hands outstretched and resting on his knees. On his face is a big smile. It was the only picture I found of him smiling this way, the corners of his eyes crinkling.

I cropped the photo to his face and emailed it to my mom.

At the funeral, several people said to us, That is such a beautiful picture of your father. Where was it taken?

We held the funeral at the Hong Kong Funeral Home. At the entrance, when we checked in, I realized there would be several funerals taking place at the same time in the building that night.

As we walked toward the room reserved for my dad, I saw a profusion of paper offerings on the floor. They were made from neon color paper: hot pink, bright yellow, lime green, silver, and gold. There were stacks and stacks of paper money, a large flat-screen television, a doll-sized Mercedes with a driver, and a cross-section of a mansion with servants inside.

Is that all for Dad? I asked.

Yes, my mom said. Later today, we'll burn it all.

We walked into the room. Facing the entrance, in the center of the opposite wall, was a large print of my dad's picture in a white wooden frame. The room was lined with white lilies from friends and relatives, with handwritten messages wishing my dad a safe journey. Flowers from my mom, my sister, and me were closest to the center. On both sides of the room, rows of white chairs faced the center aisle. In front of his picture was a large banquet table covered with fruits and roast goose and congee, more white flowers, and burning incense. We walked up to the picture and bowed three times. Some of our relatives were already sitting in the chairs, folding joss paper for burning. The paper was pale yellow, with a large gold square stamped in the middle.

You can start burning the money, one of our relatives said to me and my sister.

She showed us the door to a tiny room in the back, where there was a small fireplace, a candle, and a giant cardboard box containing all different kinds of paper money. There were imitation Hong Kong dollars, US dollars, and euros.

That's so your father can travel, the relative said.

There were also stacks of million-dollar notes, colorful circular money, and blank rectangular sheets. My sister and

I lighted a few of the bills, and threw them into the fireplace, adding more bills and stoking the flame with steel tongs.

A few minutes later, the relative came in to check on us.

You're doing it too slow! she said. Faster! Burn it faster! You can't let the flame die like that!

She moved in front of the fireplace and started doing it herself. We watched her light the paper bills and throw them into the fireplace.

There's money for you! she said. We're burning money for you!

You have to say it while you burn the paper, she told us.

Then she left the room, and my sister and I continued burning the money. As guests started to arrive, our cousins took over the burning while we welcomed the people arriving. An emcee dressed in a black suit appeared. The emcee spoke into a microphone and instructed the guests to bow to the photograph of my dad three times, and then to bow once to my mom, my sister, and me. Then, he told the three of us to lower our chins lightly in acknowledgment. Finally, the guests sat down in the chairs facing the center and began folding joss paper.

At one point, when there were no guests to acknowledge, my mom asked if we wanted to see our dad. I hadn't realized we could see him. We followed her into another small room at the back. I felt as if I'd walked into a museum. My dad lay there in his open coffin, covered with a golden yellow blanket, behind a glass window. There were spotlights shining on him. His skin was chalky and his cheeks had a pink blush.

How did they close his eyes?

We bowed.

We stood there in a row, looking at my dad through the window.

I love you, my mother said to him softly.

Later in the afternoon, a few monks arrived to carry out a Buddhist ceremony. They sat around a long table and chanted. A woman motioned for my mom, my sister, and me to offer a stick of incense to my dad and walk in a circle around the monks. We walked many circles.

In the evening, the funeral advisor announced that they would burn the large paper offerings, and that the immediate family and close relatives could attend the burning. Several of us followed him out of the building and onto the street. We walked for a few minutes until we saw a truck and a closetlike contraption for the burning. We all stood there, dressed in black, on the street under the bridge in the dark.

The funeral advisor gave us the instructions. We were to tell my dad to come receive the offerings as soon as they started burning them. We were to yell as loud as we could.

They started throwing the paper items into the burning closet.

Come get your stuff! we shouted. Come get your stuff!

The flames licked so high I wondered if the cars driving along the bridge could see them.

You're not yelling loud enough! a relative said to me. Yell louder!

It was the same one who had scolded us earlier. I wanted to throw something at her.

I yelled louder instead.

Here we were, all facing the same direction, yelling, as a man threw paper luxury items into the fire.

THE CREMATION

There was a discussion about whether I would carry out
the customs traditionally given to the eldest son. My mom
asked if I would do it. One relative told my mom that I
shouldn't because I'm not a son.

If she does it, she might never get married, the relative said.

In the end, I accepted.

On the morning after the funeral, a large group of us
returned to the funeral home. After we sat down in the
chairs and started folding more joss paper to burn, one of
the funeral advisors came over and led me into the back
room, where my dad lay in his coffin. They had moved him
from behind the window out into the viewing room.

Hold this, the advisor said, handing me a damp white towel
with both hands. Now repeat after me and say, Dad, I'm
washing your face.

I held onto both ends of the damp white towel, but the advisor didn't let go. We were both holding onto the towel now.

Dad, I'm washing your face, I said.

The advisor swept the towel back and forth in the air above my dad's face, without ever touching him. Then he asked me to go back to the main room and take a seat.

A few minutes later, they wheeled my dad out to the main room. Everyone took turns bowing in front of the coffin before sitting down again. Then they announced that they were about to close the lid of the coffin, and said that those of us born in the Year of the Horse, Rabbit, or Pig were to look away during this part of the ceremony. Because I was born in the Year of the Rabbit, I looked down at the ground. I wasn't sure when exactly they would close the coffin, so I looked down at the ground for a very long time.

Later, I carried a stone bowl filled with water over to the window. Then I carried my dad's large framed photograph to the van that took us to the cremation site.

There was a large travel bus for our relatives and family friends, and a smaller van for my mom, my sister, and me. The cremation site was at the top of a hill. The cremation was held inside, in a room covered with gold and yellow wallpaper. As we entered the room, each of us was handed a stick of incense, and we were directed to stand next to each other, row by row. My mom, my sister, and I stood at the front. The coffin sat on a conveyor belt on the left side of the room. Each of us bowed and placed our stick of incense into the burner. Then the advisor called me, my mom, and my sister over to the coffin.

Put your hand lightly on this button, he said.

We each placed a finger on the small white button on the wall.

One, two, three, he said.

We pressed the button, and the conveyor belt took the coffin, and my dad inside it, through the hole in the wall and out of the room. There were no flames and no smoke.

What's on the other side? my sister asked.

They burn him on the other side, my mom said.

In this gold and yellow room hazy with incense, the three of us pushed a button that sent my dad into flames that we could not see or smell. What did it look like on the other side? Were they going to throw the coffin into the fire the same way they threw the paper offerings into the fire? Were there rows and rows of coffins in a fluorescent room, waiting to be burned later that day?

Now that I think about it, the last time I saw my dad was when I held the damp white towel above his face. If I had known that then, I would have taken a better look.

All I thought then was, Am I holding this towel right?

SEVEN DAYS

The day after my dad died, my mom told me, The soul
returns home seven days after passing.

So Dad is coming back? I asked.

So your dad will come home next Wednesday. The funeral
advisor told us to prepare dinner for your dad, with all of
his favorite foods, and leave it out on the table before we
sleep. I thought we could have steamed rock cod, poached
chicken with ginger and scallion sauce, egg custard, and
baby bok choy. We also have to prepare three place settings,
one for your dad, one for Ox-Head, and one for Horse-Face.
They will escort your dad home and then take him away
again.

That night, I couldn't fall asleep, so I looked up Ox-Head
and Horse-Face online. Ox-Head has the head of an ox and
Horse-Face has the face of a horse. They are the guardians of
the underworld, assistants to the God of Death, taking new

souls to judgment. On one website, I saw an image of a yellowing silk scroll that depicted Ox-Head and Horse-Face scooping out the intestines from two guilty souls. Their blood dripped out in red strings.

We were not to tell my grandma that my dad died. She was still in Vancouver at this time.

If she asks how your dad is, just don't say a word, my mom said.

I didn't call my grandma for days.

Then one day, I called her, and she asked about my dad.

He's the same, I said.

I've been praying 108 times twice a day, she said. I pray that he gets better soon so he can retire and take your mom on vacations.

We didn't tell her for months, until my mom flew back to Vancouver.

Before my dad died, I'd bought *The Pocket Thich Nhat Hanh* at a bookstore and carried it with me to Hong Kong.

Dad, I bought a Buddhist book, I said. Do you want me to read it to you?

No, there's no need, he replied.

I sat next to his hospital bed, holding his hand.

Is it in English? he asked, a few minutes later.

Yes, it's in English. But I can translate it into Chinese for you. Do you want me to read it?

Okay, he said.

I took out the yellow pocket-sized book from my bag, and flipped through the first few pages. The first chapter was on

Mindfulness. I didn't know how to say mindfulness in Cantonese, so I asked him for help. I read out loud, slowly, asking him for help to translate every tenth word or so. His eyes were closed. Was I tiring him by asking him to help me translate too many words? Was he disappointed in my terrible Chinese?

I started sweating on my upper lip. I was translating it all wrong, and droplets collected inside my surgical mask. I kept reading until the nurses came in to inspect the tubes going in and out of his body. Then I closed the book and put it back into my bag.

A few days later my dad said, I learned something new from what you read to me the other day.

Really? I asked. What did you learn?

I learned that it is important to be true to yourself. Many people do whatever society tells them to do. They've lost themselves. I grew up with Confucian values, and they are limiting. I focused only on work and making a living. But I'm old now. Remember not to lose who you are.

I never got to finish reading the first chapter of *The Pocket Thich Nhat Hanh* to my dad, but we cremated the book with him because he'd said that he wanted to study Buddhism when he got better.

Six months after he died, I went back to the bookstore and bought myself another copy. In the first chapter, it says,

> You are here, alive, completely alive. That is a miracle. Some people live as though they are already dead.

Reading it now, I don't recall translating any of it.

Did you forgive him? my friend asked.

I don't know, I said. How do I know?

Then I thought of the time, a few months before he died, when we were at the hospital, and my dad was feeling a little better. We propped him up on the chair to sit for twenty minutes. He said he wanted to talk to me and my sister, so I sat on his right side holding his right hand, and my sister sat on his left side holding his left hand. He said to us, I say that I've never hit either of you, but it's not true. I have. He turned to my sister and said, You were little and you refused to take a bath. You were running around, misbehaving. So I spanked you. Then he turned to look at me and said, You were older, probably fourteen, and walking around so quietly that you scared me. So I hit your head. I had told you not to walk around so quietly like that. You did it anyway. But you probably don't remember any of this, either of you. It was so long ago.

I remember, I said.

I remember too, my sister said.

I think he was reaching out for forgiveness then, that day at
the hospital, and I didn't want to give it to him. I didn't
want to forgive him, and now I haven't forgiven myself for
not forgiving him when he needed it. He just wanted
forgiveness, and I didn't give it to him.

But can you forgive yourself now? my friend asked.

I don't know. I don't know how.

TOES

I can still see my dad's toes.

His big toes rounded into a circle above the joint, as mine do. Long black hairs fanned out below.

He rubbed his big toe and his second toe back and forth against each other, a soft pattering, while watching the news, while reading the paper, while staring out the window.

Sometimes I rub my toes back and forth so I can make that sound too.

I read an article this morning, a doctor wrote it, I said. It was about a piano teacher at the end of her life. The doctor wasn't her doctor. His kid was her student, and they had become friends, in a way.

Why did he write the article? my sister asked.

He said that despite having worked in medicine for over a decade, he still didn't know what to do when a patient seemed incurable. Do they do everything they can to keep her alive? Or should she give up? And why are these the two main options? So he asked her what her fears were, and when she said more pain, humiliation, and loss of bodily control, he suggested she try hospice. Back in her home, they set up everything she needed in the living room, and adjusted her medication until she was comfortable yet aware. Then, they asked her what it would mean for her to have her best possible day. In the end, she started teaching piano lessons again, and former students flew in from around the country to perform a concert for her. She said goodbye to all of her students, and died peacefully soon after.

Does that make you think about Dad?

It makes me think about the infusions, the tubes, the cuts, the ventilator. I can still hear the sound of that ventilator breathing after he died. Why didn't I say something? Why didn't I ask Dad what he wanted? When he first admitted himself to the hospital, he thought he would be there for only a month and he was there for almost a year until he died. But then I also think, I didn't know any better, how was I supposed to know? And why didn't the doctors say something to us? Why didn't they tell us what his chances really were?

But maybe he wanted to live. You know those stories about old couples, all their hair has gone white, one of them dies and the other dies not long after. Dad probably could have let go a lot earlier if he had wanted to.

I guess so.

What do you think Dad's best possible day would have been like?

DREAM

Last night I had a dream.

In the dream, my dad's face surfaced. It was healthy, and blurry around the edges.

He spoke to me without making a sound.

I chose to die, he said.

I woke up, with warm tears running down my face, forming a cool damp patch against my cheek on the pillow.

Then I fell asleep again.

AN EMAIL FROM MY DAD

While cleaning out old emails, I stumbled upon one from my dad, dated November 2006. I was in my second year of college then, applying for summer internships, worried about finding the right one for my future.

He wrote:

> I am very happy to receive your e-mail. The letter you wrote to your grandma in Chinese is excellent. Although there are mistakes, you actually improve a lot and master the language and vocabulary confidently and beautifully.
>
> I have said before that the first or second job is not important and may not be your future career. Sometimes you may think or wander but don't be too serious—especially for the summer job. We easily change. Study and enjoy!

I stared at the screen. I had no memory of reading this email.

Why did I remember only his disappointment in me?

Did I ever get to know who he was becoming? Did I try?

A MEMORY

There is a memory I can revisit only in pieces.

I am standing in the hospital.

My dad is sitting up in his bed.

Somehow, no one else is in the room.

There is a square of yellow sunlight on the floor, a small suitcase by my feet.

Outside, a taxi is waiting.

In this life, my dad says.

His voice cracks. He turns his face away from me.

In this life, he says, it is one of my greatest fortunes that I was blessed with two daughters.

HOME

After my dad died, my mom's lungs collapsed again for the first time in thirty years.

She sold our childhood home in Vancouver, said goodbye to our family friends, and returned to Hong Kong with my grandma.

Though it was hard when they first immigrated, after living there for over two decades, my mom and my grandma both grew to prefer Vancouver. The green, the quiet. The temperate winters and mediterranean summers. The air is so fresh in Canada, they said. But since my sister and I moved away for school and work, they found no reason to stay anymore.

I said, I thought you liked living in Vancouver. Why are you moving back to Hong Kong?

My mom replied, What else am I supposed to do?

I once asked my dad, If you could live anywhere in the world, where would you live?

He said, I don't want to live anywhere else. I like Hong Kong. It is my home.

My mom says that for a few years after we immigrated to Vancouver, every time my dad left for the airport, I cried.

One time, a day or two after he flew back to Hong Kong, my mom volunteered to work as a translator at the community center registration evening. She signed up for it because she thought it would be a chance to learn something new.

I don't remember this, but my mom says that night as she walked toward the door, I started to wail. I tugged at her clothes and begged her not to go. She told me that she would be back soon, that she would be right back, she was only going to the community center for a few hours. But I cried and cried, I cried so hard that my grandma had to hold me back as my mom stepped outside and locked the door.

I think that at some point along the way, maybe in that moment, I collapsed proximity with love.

And as I got older, I kept moving and moving—from Vancouver to Providence to London to New York—because whenever I started to feel attached to a place or to people, I wanted, subconsciously, to make sure I would be the first to leave.

These days, my relatives say, Hurry up and come back to Hong Kong. Why do you leave your mother all alone?

And I am overcome with envy for the people who live where they were born and raised. Why is it that I have to choose?

HAIR CEREMONY

While cleaning out my dad's closet in our apartment in
Hong Kong, my mom found a box of tapes, shot with the
giant black handheld recorder my parents used in the
eighties and nineties.

In the thick humidity of Hong Kong, some of the tapes grew
mold over the years, like little snowflakes blossoming on
the surface of the film. Some of them were damaged and
had to be thrown out. Of the remaining footage, many of
the colors faded, creating beautiful tinges of pink, blue, and
green that shine out of nowhere.

My mom asked her friend to digitize the footage, and brought
it on a thumb drive to New York, where I was now living.

In one video, dated October 1986, my mom sits in a wicker
chair, wearing pink poplin pajamas with a white bib collar.
She looks ahead at a mirror on the table in front of her,
head tipped slightly forward, as her sister-in-law wraps a

cypress leaf into her hair with red string. It is the night before my parents' wedding in Hong Kong, and my mom is not yet twenty-seven.

Are you already filming? my mom asks.

I'm filming! my uncle shouts from behind the camera.

I'll smile prettier, then, my mom says, and her face breaks into a grin.

Off-screen, my grandma chuckles. Then one of our elder female relatives steps forward and picks up two wooden combs. As she runs them through my mom's hair, she says:

Yat so, so dou mei,
The first comb, combs to the end,
(May your marriage last a lifetime)

Yi so, ji syun mun dei,
The second comb, to have children and grandchildren everywhere,
(May you be blessed with children and grandchildren)

Saam so, baak faat chai mei!
The third comb, for white hair and white eyebrows!
(May you be blessed with longevity)

My mom bobs her head happily as everyone claps and cheers. Then two hands appear in the camera frame, placing two Coca-Cola cans on the table. In each red can stands a flaming red candlestick.

Now what happens? my uncle's voice asks.

Now we wait until they burn to the end, someone replies.

That's going to take so long! my uncle says.

No, it won't take long. It won't take long at all, someone else replies.

As the video clip ends, the room is full of the warm chatter and laughter of my mom and her family.

The night before my own wedding in New York, my mom came to my apartment with a set of hair ceremony tools that she brought over from Hong Kong.

Laid out on top of a red piece of card paper and wrapped in flimsy clear plastic, the set had two red dragon phoenix wax candles on wooden sticks, a pair of scissors with shiny golden handles, a red ruler, a mirror with a handle wrapped in red brocade, a spool of green thread, a spool of red thread, and a round wooden comb.

I asked my sister to film it for me.

In the video, I sit in a gray chair, wearing a pale pink T-shirt and pink and white striped boxer shorts, facing an open window where I can see the moon. On the coffee table in front of me, all the items from the hair ceremony set are laid out. The pair of red wax candles stand upright in an empty jam jar, flaming.

Beside me, my mom bows three times. Then she places three glowing joss sticks into the jam jar next to the candles. Pinching a bobby pin between her thumb and forefinger, she slides a cypress leaf with red string into my hair. Then she leans back to take a better look, tucks some of my hair behind my ear, and hands me the mirror wrapped in red brocade. Thank you, I say. I hold the mirror with both hands. She picks up the wooden comb, smiling, and says, You're grown up now. I wish you good health and happiness in your life.

According to tradition, the bride is meant to look at her own reflection in the mirror all throughout the hair ceremony. But as my mom slid the comb through my hair, I couldn't help but angle the mirror so that I could look at her face instead, so attentive, as she recited the same three blessings given to her thirty years before.

TEA CEREMONY

My grandma flew to New York for my wedding too, but she missed my hair ceremony. She was at her hotel, jet-lagged from the sixteen-hour flight, resting.

For years, whenever we talked on the phone, I would say to my grandma, You have to take care of your health so that you can see me walk down the aisle!

And she would say, I know, I'm taking my vitamins every day. I hope you get married soon so I can meet your baby!

Then she would let out her low-pitched cackle.

The day before the wedding, we held an unconventional tea ceremony, as my family and my husband's family gathered together in our apartment. Since my husband's family is not Chinese, one of my aunts explained every step in Cantonese, then I translated it into English for them.

One after another, our elder relatives took turns sitting on the couch, sometimes as a couple and sometimes as an individual, as my husband and I, kneeling on bright red cushions on the floor, offered them pu'erh tea.

Two of my aunts stationed themselves by the kitchen sink, washing the teacups after every round, and my younger cousin scuttled back and forth with a tray, taking away the used teacups and bringing us fresh ones.

When it was finally time for my mom's turn, as she sat down on the couch alone, I couldn't help but imagine my dad beside her.

And when it was my grandma's turn, as she lowered herself onto the couch, I was struck by how small her body was, surprised by how fragile it appeared in the moment that as I lifted her a full teacup with both my hands, I couldn't stop the tears from running.

GRANDMOTHERS

My grandma says that, of all the people she has known in her life, she misses her grandma the most. She says, I cared about her, but I didn't know how to appreciate her. She was kind and hardworking, and she suffered so much. But I asked her to cook for me even when she was very old.

When my grandma tells me this, she is staring at the ground, her gray-white hair backlit against the sunny window. I feel, in that moment, a feeling I cannot put into words. As silly as it sounds, it somehow never occurred to me you could miss someone when you're that old. She has missed her grandma for over fifty years, and that is so much longer than I have been alive.

A STICK OF INCENSE

After the wedding, my husband and I flew to Hong Kong and went with my mom to the columbarium where my dad's urn is housed. By the entrance, a shop sold all kinds of paper offerings, from clothing to sports cars to abalone and roast goose. We picked out a green sweater, a white button-down, gray pants, and brown Converse shoes.

Among the wall of little portraits, we found the picture of my dad, the one I took of him at the beach all those years ago, the one where his eyes crinkle. We each lit a stick of incense for him and bowed three times. Then we went over to the furnace to burn his new outfit.

Come get your stuff! my mom and I shouted, as my husband stoked the flames.

SO MANY QUESTIONS

There are so many questions I want to ask my dad.

What were you like when you were a kid?

What are the things you wish you'd known?

What makes you sad?

And what makes you happy?

People ask me why I've been recording my mother's and grandmother's stories.

I asked them questions only after my dad died.

THE HALLWAY

There is a memory I held against my mom for years, one that took place in our childhood home in Vancouver. In this memory, our house is dark except for the dimly lit hallway between my mom's room and the bathroom. She and I are standing in this hallway, and I am looking up at her, the lightbulb above us casting deep shadows down her face.

She screams at me, and I don't know what I have done wrong. She yells, I should just die! If I die early, your life would be better, wouldn't it!

For years, I thought, why would anyone ever say that to a child?

Only recently did I think to ask my mom what it was like to give birth in a foreign land, so far away from her husband, to a baby that wasn't expected to live.

MY MOM SAYS:

After your sister was born, the nurses drew her blood
every day for testing. Since she didn't have enough
platelets, she bruised wherever they poked the needle, and,
after a while, her skin was purple all over. So they shaved
off some of her hair and drew from her head.

Then the nurse said they would have to put in a central
venous line. After they gave your sister a platelet infusion,
they took her downstairs for the surgery. I waited upstairs, I
didn't know why it was taking so long. Then they told me
they'd given her too much anesthesia, so she was still asleep.

Your aunt came to Vancouver to help me. She stayed
overnight in the hospital to watch over your sister, so I
could sleep in my own bed. One day, she saw that a nurse
accidentally pulled out the central line by one or two inches
while cleaning the area. Your aunt started crying because
she was so scared. The doctor said they would need to give
her another platelet infusion and redo the surgery.

Platelet infusion is very painful, more painful than blood. Your sister screamed so loudly.

After we got home from the hospital, I sterilized the central line every day and replaced the gauze and tape. You have to keep it really clean because it can get infected. I was so afraid of dirtiness. If I went out and bought a box of tissues, I wiped the box with rubbing alcohol as soon as I got home. I washed my hands all the time. I was like that for a few years.

Every day I waited for the results of the blood test. Your dad was in Hong Kong, he was very worried, and every day he called me and asked for the report. But sometimes the hospital didn't have the results ready, and whenever I didn't have an answer for your dad, he got mad at me.

During this period, I got angry easily. Sometimes my brain thought, I need to leave this place, I need to go away.

When your sister was two and a half and fully recovered, we went back to Hong Kong for the first time since immigrating. Your dad still lived with his mother and sister in their old apartment, and that apartment was so dirty. The two of you slept on the floor next to our bed, and you stepped all over the blankets with your dirty feet. I worried your sister would get an infection. So I decided to mop the floors myself. The first time I mopped the floors, the bucket of water turned black, so I mopped it a second time, and the water was still black, so I mopped it a third time. I barely slept because your sister was jet-lagged and ran around the apartment in the middle of the night. I remember one night I followed her into the kitchen, and when I turned on the light, cockroaches scattered across the floor, and your sister started crying. Then she got chicken pox too. I was so tired, looking after the two of you. That summer I threw stuff and punched the bed.

All day, your dad was at work. One evening, he came home from work and we took the two of you out to have dinner at Snow Garden Restaurant. There was a long wait, so I decided to stand outside by myself. I was so tired from mopping that my legs felt like jelly. Your dad came outside to ask me what I was doing.

When he saw that I was upset, he got upset at me. Who was more upset? We sat through dinner competing.

When did you get better? I asked.

My mom said, Back then, I was always thinking, I don't want to stay here, I want to go somewhere where I am alone and there is nobody else. I think I was better after I stopped having those thoughts. I don't know when it was. I never saw any doctors because I didn't know there was anything wrong with me. Nobody noticed either. I only realized later, years after I'd gotten better.

Did Dad know about it?

I didn't tell him and he didn't ask me. We only spent time together once a year when we came back to Hong Kong for the summers, and every time he got angry at me about something. Every year I wanted to tell him, and every year I waited to do it. Then I didn't have the chance to tell him anymore. That's why I want to say something to you now. I see you only once a year, and every time you get angry at me about something, just like your dad did. I know everyone has different tempers, so I haven't held it against you. I'm not blaming myself and I'm not blaming you either. I know very little. I didn't get as much education as you, so if I do something wrong, you can tell me and we can talk about it. It's very hard when you get angry at me every time we see each other. I never got the chance to tell your dad, so now I'm telling you. I don't want to keep it in my heart. We spend so little time together, why not spend it happily? I wasn't going to say anything, since I knew you wouldn't want to hear it, but then you've been asking me all these questions about the past.

Thank you for telling me.

Don't cry, it's already in the past. I knew you would cry right away.

Thank you for telling me.

I knew you would get upset at me for saying this. That's why I didn't want to tell you. I knew you would get upset.

I'm not upset at you. I'm crying because I'm sorry.

I haven't blamed you. Every generation is like this. You see how I get angry at your grandma all the time too. I can't help it. But I'm trying to change.

SLEEP

Sometimes I think about what I would do if my dad were alive today.

I love you, I would say.

I wouldn't care if he said it back or not.

I would hug him.

I would put my arm around him while he watched the news.

I would tell him about my husband.

Can't wait for you to meet him, I would say.

I would finish reading *The Pocket Thich Nhat Hanh* to him.

Remember that time you yelled at me and slammed the door because I didn't address you when I called you? I would say.

I forgive you for everything, I would say.

I would wake him up at sunrise.

It would be his birthday, and he would be turning sixty-three.

We would practice tai chi in the morning light.

I would slice papaya for us on a plate. We would eat it on the balcony.

I would boil hot water and steep osmanthus tea.

We would study translations of the Heart Sutra, mine in English and his in Chinese.

Emptiness is form, I would say. What does that mean?

If you think you understand, then you probably don't understand, he would say. He would shake his head and chuckle.

We would listen to jazz.

This album is *Solo Monk,* I would say.

And my dad would nod his head.

I would take him out for dim sum.

We would eat for hours, and then we would go for a walk.

Isn't it a beautiful day? I would say.

Look at how green it is, I would say.

I would ask him if he was in the mood for ice cream, and because he'd said he would be more carefree once he got better, we would share three scoops of ice cream in a cup.

I would choose pistachio, vanilla, and black sesame.

This ice cream is not bad, he would say, but it would be perfect if it felt less cold on my teeth.

I would laugh, and then we would continue on our walk, maybe with a puppy because he would want a puppy in his life.

We would stop by the beach and watch the sun sink into the sea.

Then we would head home, where my mom and sister would be on the beige couch watching television together, and my grandma would be eating mango and resting her feet.

We would walk in the door, and the puppy would run over and scramble up on my sister's lap.

What should we eat for dinner? my dad would say, as we slipped our heels out of our shoes.

You four decide, my grandma would say.

What do you two want to eat for dinner? my mom would ask.

I don't know, my sister would say.

Anything, I would say.

Let's eat pizza, my dad would say.

Then we would sit around the dinner table with boxes of hot pizza, the cheese seeping grease stains into the cardboard.

We would eat until we were stuffed, and then we would have strawberry cheesecake for dessert.

Then we would all sit close together on the couch, turn on the television, and listen to the hum of the news as we sank into its lull.

I'm ready to sleep, my dad would say, and we would peel ourselves off the couch.

Good night! we would say.

I would stand there, and watch my dad walk into his room before he fell into a long, deep, and wonderful sleep.

And I would say, I love you! as I clicked off each light in our home.

ACKNOWLEDGMENTS

To my sister, Pik-Tone: You read a million drafts with boundless compassion. Thank you for your big heart and your keen intuition, for being my first reader and my life buddy since you were born. When I write, I write to you.

To Julia Masnik, my wise and gentle guide: Thank you for the wonder and the play, for being by my side on every step of this journey and always knowing what I need. My gratitude to Gloria Loomis and the Watkins/Loomis Agency.

To Nicole Counts, my loving and ingenious editor: Thank you for believing in me, challenging me, and seeing what I couldn't see. You've been my champion since the day we met, and I've grown so much in your care.

I am deeply grateful to Chris Jackson, Mika Kasuga, Ada Yonenaka, Greg Mollica, Avideh Bashirrad, Madison Dettlinger, Jess Bonet, Carla Bruce-Eddings, and the rest of the incredible team at One World and Random House. My heartfelt thanks to Simon Sullivan for the gorgeous design, and to Donna Cheng for a cover I love beyond words.

To Jordan Ginsberg, my brilliant Canadian editor, and the Strange Light team: Thank you for welcoming me and giving this book a place in my home country.

To Holly Tavel: How lucky I was to get a spot in your class fifteen years ago. Thank you for instilling confidence in me and encouraging me to write this book.

To Morgan Ross: Words cannot express the gratitude I feel for you. Thank you for your generosity and your discerning eye, for reading draft after draft and helping me shape the empty space of this book over and over.

To Peter von Ziegesar: Your enthusiasm for every version of this book has buoyed me in the most difficult of times. Thank you for always cheering me on.

To Daniel Goldbard and Autumn Graham: Thank you for reading early drafts, for the flowers and the dinners, for celebrating all my acceptances and rejections with equal exuberance.

To Jyothi Natarajan, Yasmin Majeed, and everyone at the Asian American Writers' Workshop: You opened all the doors for me. Thank you for nourishing me and accepting me with open arms. Thank you to Anelise Chen and *The Margins,* for editing and publishing my first story, *Ghost Forest,* which grew into this book. And thank you to my fierce fellowship cohort, Ayesha Raees, Jen Lue, and Zena Agha for the magical, transformational year.

I am thankful for my teachers who read excerpts and shared invaluable feedback: Sophie McManus, Mike Scalise, Bushra Rehman, and Padma Viswanathan. Thank you to Ava Chin for the pep talks, and to T Kira Madden for rooting for me. Thank you, Catherine Chung, for writing me an inspiring mentor, and then becoming one too.

I am grateful to the Millay Colony and to the singular Metatron Press for the early support. To my Kundiman Retreat and Mentorship Lab family: Thank you for being my community.

Thank you to Kiyomi Dong, Diana Geman-Wollach, and Mallory Kotik for giving me insightful feedback on my seedling pages. Thank you to Stephanie Liu and Natalie Fu for the illuminating conversations about astronaut families. And thank you to the friends whose encouragement kept me going over the years, especially Elsa Duré, Hillary Harnett, Ruby Shah, Michael Glassman, Rahul Keerthi, Nathanael Geman, Neha Zope, Neerav Parekh, Abhay Sagar, Mannan Jalan, Paolo Servado, Valeria Dröge, Alison Kuo and Williamson Brasfield, Eric Huang, Amanda Ajamfar, Emma Eisenberg, Amanda Huynh, Kathie Halfin, and Heesun Shin.

To Pinky-Z Wu: Amy Haejung, Annina Zheng-Hardy, Kyle Lucia Wu (for being my caring pub buddy), and K-Ming Chang (for paddling the kayak ahead with verve). I'm so happy we found each other.

To Uncle Frank, Auntie Kathy, Yi, and Grace: I'm so grateful for your kindness.

To Auntie Garis, Uncle Ben, and Billy: Thank you for your love and care.

To my in-laws, especially Lily, Ollie, Julie, and Kevin: What a joy it is to be in your boisterous and endlessly doting family.

To my aunts, uncles, and cousins, especially Wah E, Kinyi, Uncle Edric and Aunt Linda: Thank you for your love and unwavering devotion. Thank you, Uncle 9, for always looking out for me.

To my father, a visionary, the wisest person I knew: It is one of my greatest fortunes that you were my dad.

To my mother, the most kindhearted person I know: You are the epitome of courage, persistence, and selflessness. Thank you for going to the ends of the earth to support me in everything I do.

婆婆，多謝您對我的照顧和關愛。您是我心目中最有創意的人。

And to Ben: In your love, at last I found my home.

PIK-SHUEN FUNG is a Canadian writer and artist living in New York City. She is the recipient of fellowships and residencies from the Asian American Writers' Workshop, Kundiman, the Millay Colony, and Storyknife. *Ghost Forest* is her first book.

pikshuen.com

ABOUT THE TYPE

This book is set in Spectrum, a typeface designed
in the 1940s and the last from the distinguished
Dutch type designer Jan van Krimpen (1892–1958).
Spectrum is a polished and reserved font.